OTHER BOOKS BY WILLIAM POST

A CHANGE IN
TRADITION

WILLIAM POST

authorHOUSE

AuthorHouse™
1663 Liberty Drive
Bloomington, IN 47403
www.authorhouse.com
Phone: 1 (800) 839-8640

Published by AuthorHouse 08/16/2017

ISBN: 978-1-5462-0419-0 (sc)
ISBN: 978-1-5462-0418-3 (e)

CONTENTS

PREFACE

This is a story about a young man, Kellen Keller, who breaks from the tradition of his father and grandfather to live a different life. His father had only one goal in life and that was to own the largest ranch in Texas. It becomes an obsession with him.

His mother helped form Kel's life to one who follows Christ. She also sees that he takes piano lessons. He has a real talent for the piano, and that serves him admirably through his life.

His school in Marble Falls has a forward thinking school board that also helps form Kel's life. After high school his father takes him to help him on his ranch. His older brothers were taken when they were in their early teens, but Kel's mother would not let her husband take Kel until he finished high school.

On the ranch, Kel is partnered with an older man who teaches him everything about being a cowboy. As Kel's hands are quick from running scales on the piano, he learns to draw and shoot a pistol to the point that he is deadly.

A shooting incident, ends his ranch life, and Kel leaves the ranch for San Antonio where he becomes a deputy sheriff.

He is good at detective work, and makes a name for himself. However, he sees that he doesn't want a life in law enforcement.

He leaves for Austin to go to college. He is reunited with his mother and her new husband. She divorces her husband because he only sees her a couple of weeks out of the year as he is engrossed with his three ranches.

At Kel's first day of college, he meets three women who are seeking to be lawyers like himself. They form a group and become devoted to one another all through college. After they pass the bar examination they open a law firm in Austin.

Rumors of war between the states changes Kel's life. He does not hold with slavery, and the group advises him to go East before the war starts. He does that, and opens another career. His experiences in Texas serve him well as he has many adventures.

A Change in Tradition blends historical facts with fiction. Exact events may be a bit convoluted with the fiction, but is not varied too far from history.

CHAPTER 1
THE KELLY FAMILY

The Kelly family lived east of Bishop, Missouri and The Turners lived on the west side. No one knew how the feud started, but everyone knew it was there. In town there was a bar on the west side of town where the Turner's drank. There was also a bar on the east side of town where the Kelly men did their drinking.

The only time they saw one another was at the general store owned by Hank Divot. If the Turner's were buying supplies, the Kelly's stayed out until the Turner's were through shopping, and visa versa. However, at school, children from both families attended the same school and seemed to get along. That is where John Kelly met Betty Turner. They never said much to each other, but each knew they were liked by the other. So it went through their years of school.

John Kelly knew his father would never agree to him marrying Betty, and she knew that her father, Donald, would never agree to having John Kelly as a son-in-law. It was a hopeless situation.

Both were seventeen and would be graduating, soon. John knew he would never see Betty again unless he made an arrangement with her. A day before graduation, John whispered to Betty, "Meet me behind the girl's outhouse after school."

Betty was there when John arrived. John said, "I know we never talked much, but I want you to be my girl. If you feel the same, we need to find somewhere to meet. Do you want to meet with me?"

"Yes, I do. I know this feud business runs deeply with my father and yours, but it's not our business. I have nothing against you Kelly's."

"I feel the same, Betty. I like you a lot, and the only way we can be together is to find somewhere to meet. We can then talk and figure out how we can be together."

"How about under the Bethel Bridge. I can leave my buggy in the woods, and you could come down the creek and meet me there."

"What day and what time?"

"I do shopping on Thursdays. I could come at lunchtime, and we could have an hour together. Do you think you can slip down the creek unnoticed?"

"Yeah. I will leave my horse in town, and go down a wash I know, then meet you there." So it began. They met every Thursday and fell in love.

This went on for a year before Myrtle Riddle saw John go down the wash, and wondered where he was going. She was sweet on John, although he never gave her the time of day. She began watching him, and sure enough, every Thursday John would descend into that wash, and disappear for up to an hour.

The Riddle family was not connected to the feud, but

they held mostly to the Kelly family as they went to the same church. The Turner family held their own services at home.

After several times of watching John go down that wash at precisely noon every Thursday, Myrtle decided to see what he was up to. The next Thursday at about eleven thirty, Myrtle went down the wash. She crossed the creek, and hid behind a thick bush. She waited, and could hear John coming. She watched him turn, and go under the Bethel bridge. From her perch, she could see Betty Turner descend the side of the bridge, and meet John. They talked some, then began to kiss and hold one another. Their wooing never went beyond that, as there was no place to sit.

Myrtle was jealous. She wanted John, but now Betty Turner had him. She decided to write a note to Cecil Turner, Betty's brother, and inform on them. She wrote out what she had observed, and left the note signed only as, "A Friend."

After receiving the note, Cecil took it to his father, Donald Turner. Donald studied the note thinking it was probably not true, but he wanted to make sure. He sent Cecil to follow Betty the next Thursday. Cecil saw her descend the slope. He found a place where he could see under the bridge. John arrived a moment later, and they began petting. Cecil reported this to his Dad.

Donald began thinking. He had a cousin, Lester Turner, who had lost his wife some five years ago. He had inherited a good farm next to his, and he always coveted a piece of Lester's farm that would enhance his own farm a great deal. A plan then began to form in his mind. If he could get Lester to agree to give him the portion of land he wanted, he would give him Betty as a wife.

Lester was fifteen years older than Betty, but it was quite common for a man's second wife to be much younger. Lester was no prize. He wore a beard and a mustache. His beard was stained with tobacco juice, and he seldom changed clothes or took a bath. He stank so badly that even the saloon girls would have nothing to do with him. It was said that he now used cows to relieve his desire.

Donald went to Lester and laid out his proposition. Lester had seen Betty, and she was a good looking woman and young. He wasn't quick to answer, but studied the proposition. On one hand, he wanted a woman to cook, clean and keep up his house. On the other hand, he knew how contrary women could be. His first wife lasted only two years. It was said that a shotgun she was putting away went off and killed her. Actually she had put the barrel in her mouth and pulled the trigger.

The Turners and the Kelleys mostly looked at their wives as property. They were to do all the house chores, bear and raise the children. Each Turner man ruled his family with an iron fist, and what he said went. If anyone objected, the person brought the wrath of the father or husband down on them. It was an understood rule that no one violated. Donald's wife, Sissy, had left him after ten years of marriage. No one knew what happened to her. She had saved her money for ten years. Her plan was to leave when she accumulated a hundred dollars.

Sissy went into Bishop for supplies on Thursday. Betty always went with her, but Betty was ill with a bad cold. She told Betty she needed to see her cousin who lived south of

Bishop and would be late coming home. Sissy wasn't home by supper, so Betty got up and fixed the meal.

Donald asked why Sissy was not there, and Betty explained she was visiting her cousin who was ill, and probably spent the night. She said this to keep her father from a rant he often did when things didn't suit him. The day turned into three and Donald went to see the cousin. Of course Sissy had never gone there. She had driven southwest to Springfield. She traveled all day and all night. She made a bed in the buggy and slept four hours then traveled on.

She only passed through Springfield and traveled on to Joplin. There she got a job as a waitress in a café. She met a farmer at the church she attended, and married him a year later. No one in Bishop ever saw her again.

***

Some years back, John went over to his granddad's farm. He didn't find him at the house, so he went to the barn. He could see his grandfather moving some equipment around, and looking into an old churn. He then put the equipment back in place. John waited until he had finished that chore, then acted like he had just come up and called for his grandfather. His grandfather said, "In here, John."

A month later, John went to his grandfather's farm when he was sure his grandfather was not at home. He moved the equipment, and looked into the old churn. It was half full of money, some gold coins, but mostly folding money. It looked like a fortune to John. He put everything back in place and left. He never mentioned this to anyone.

Just after he graduated from high school his grandfather died. While they were carrying his grandfather from the church to the graveyard, John rode his horse over to his grandfather's barn. He moved the equipment to see if the money was still there. To John's delight it was. John took a gunnysack, and put the money in it, and rode away. He had a secret place under the Bethel Bridge to hide things he hid from his father. His father didn't want anyone to have anything private. John had a hunting knife, a pistol and scabbard he kept there. He had traded a pig for the pistol and hunting knife to a family traveling through Bishop. He hid his grandfather's money under the bridge, then rode off to the burial. He wanted to count the money, but didn't have the time.

An incident had occurred between the Turner's and the Kelly's. It seems Thurl Kelly had ridden his horse into town too fast, and had hit one of the children of Levell Turner. The child was skinned up pretty badly, but otherwise unhurt. Instead of stopping and helping the child, Thurl just yelled at the kid for being in the way.

Even though the wedding was planned for the next day between Betty and Lester, a meeting was called to evaluate how best to handle the Thurl Kelly situation.

That afternoon while John was about to get on his horse, Myrtle came up to him and said, "Have you heard the news?"

"What news," John asked.

"Betty Turner is marrying her cousin Lester tomorrow. However, the Turners are meeting tonight at Lester's house to decide what they're going to do to Thurl for riding into

Morris Turner, yesterday. However, it shouldn't delay the wedding. What do you think of that?"

John's mind started thinking. He looked at Myrtle and said, "It doesn't matter to me, I'm leaving in the morning for Virginia. I've hired on as a horse groom at a stable near Lynchburg. What do you think of that?"

Myrtle's mouth dropped open.

John said, "Now promise me you won't tell a soul, Myrtle. Will you promise?"

"Oh yes, John. Thank you for confiding in me. It will be our secret. Will you be back before Christmas?"

"Yeah, I wouldn't miss Christmas at home."

John then left. He thought if he could get Betty to go with him, she could use her buggy with his horse tied behind, and go to Texas with him. He had heard there were cattle running wild down there. You could homestead the land, and use the open range for your cattle.

He rode home and told his dad about the Turner's meeting to retaliate on the Kelly's for what Thurl had done. He then said, "I've been offered a job for a couple of months in Lynchburg. Can I go, now that the crops are in?"

His father was thinking about the Turner's as it was serious to him, and said, "Oh, yeah, go ahead." His father then left to meet with the Kelly families' leaders.

It was turning dark and John rode by the bridge, and picked up his pistol, knife and money. He then rode to Betty's farm. He could hear horses coming, and rode off the trail, and into the trees. He could tell it was Donald Turner and some of his kin riding to Lester's house.

He reached Betty's farm and called to her. She came out immediately and said, "Dad's not here, so it's okay."

John got down and said, "Betty I heard about your father making you marry Lester tomorrow. Hitch up your buggy I'm taking you to Texas." She flew into his arms and kissed him.

She then said, "I'll leave a note that says Lyndell came and asked me to go help Emma, as the baby is due any day now."

Her sister, Emma had married a man from Kentucky, some sixty miles north of Bishop. Everyone knew Emma was pregnant.

Betty hurriedly wrote the note. She began throwing her clothes into a valise with her toiletries. She then packed them food for the trip. While she was doing that, John was harnessing her horse to her buggy. He threw in a fifty pound sack of oats, and tied his horse behind the buggy. He then drove the buggy around to the front. By this time, Betty had placed several blankets and two pillows, along with her trappings, and the food on the porch. They placed it all in the boot of the buggy. Betty jumped up and they were off.

As they traveled John told Betty about telling his father he was going to a job in Virginia. He then laughed and said, "I told Myrtle about me going to Virginia. I told her not to tell a soul as it was a secret. You know that secret will become like building up steam in a steam engine. She will get so full, she can't help but blab it."

Betty laughed and said, "That was smart. She has a crush on you, and told several people she did. She will want to tell people that you confided in her because you like her so much. I can just see her telling everyone she meets. She will tell them, then make them promise not to tell anyone, but everyone will know it by the end of the week."

John said, "She also told me that your father had called a meeting at Lester's house to decide what to do about Thurl's riding over Morris, yesterday. He will want some revenge. That gave me the idea of getting you, and going to Texas.

"We will change our names. From this day forward, call me by my middle name, Alton, and I will call you by your middle name Louise. When we marry, our last name will be Keller instead of Kelly. Mr. Alton and Louise Keller. What do you say?"

"I say I'm marrying a very smart man who I love very much."

Betty's father found the note when he returned, and didn't think much of it. She could marry Lester anytime. If Emma needed her, she needed her. He would tell Lester that the wedding had to be postponed for a couple of weeks.

At the meeting they had decided to just shoot one of Kelly's cows, and let it go at that.

***

They drove all night long. He let Betty sleep that night. The next day, she drove the buggy and he slept. By night fall they were both bushed. They found a good camping spot, and slept the entire night.

The next day he told Louise about his grandfather's money. He said, "I have never counted it. When we stop tonight we'll count it. That money will give us a start in Texas. I have heard there are many cows just running loose in the Southwestern part of the state. If we go to a Texas land office, we can ask them, and get an idea where we should head. I want to be a rancher."

"Just so we are away from Missouri. That feud between the Turner's and the Kelly's has gone on for a hundred years, and for what? Hate is a terrible thing. Daddy preaches the love of Christ, but his heart is filled with hate. He treated mama so badly, that she ran off. No one ever found out where she went. She just left, and no one ever found out. The Turner men treat their women like property. They say that Lester's wife had an accident, but I overheard daddy telling Uncle Charlie, that he believes she killed herself. I do too. When daddy told me he had given me to Lester, I began thinking of using that shotgun, too."

"Let's not talk about the past, Louise. From here out, we're Texans heading for our destiny."

CHAPTER 2

THE TRIP TO TEXAS

The next night when they stopped, they counted the money. It came to two thousand, four hundred and eighty one dollars. Alton didn't think there was half that amount. He looked at Louise and said, "I wish I hadn't counted the money. I thought it was less than half that amount. Now I'm worried someone will rob us."

"You know that tin box I brought with my keepsakes in it? Let's put two hundred dollars in it. Then you build a hiding place in the buggy that no one can get to, unless they dismantle the buggy."

"That's a real good idea, Louise. I'll go over to the buggy now, and look for a place. If someone robs us, they'll think that the money in the tin box is all the money we have."

Alton left for the buggy. After about ten minutes he saw where he could pullout an iron bar, then raise the entire flooring up. It took some time, but with Louise helping, they were able to hide the money.

They were ready to go to bed and Louise said, "Are we going to make love before we are married." Alton said, "No." We will start this union right. We'll get married at the first town we come to. Then, if your pa shows up, he can't separate us."

"You don't know pa, he'll kill you on sight."

"Thanks for telling me. If I see him first, I'll make you an orphan."

"He won't catch us. He'll believe I'm at Emma's for over two weeks. By that time, we'll be in Texas looking for a ranch to buy."

Three days later, they came to Fort Smith Arkansas, and were married. They spent the night in a hotel and stayed for two days, mostly in their hotel room. Louise found that Alton wasn't much of a lover. He was like many of the men in her family, and knew nothing of how to treat a woman.

***

At Christmas Alton had not returned and his father became worried. After New Years, he decided to go to Lynchburg, Virginia to find his son. He asked every farm in a fifty mile radius of Lynchburg, but no one had ever heard of John Kelly. After a week he began to think about what could have happened.

He knew about his sparking Betty Turner and thought, *"Donald Turner would never permit his daughter to leave with Betty."* He then dismissed the idea of them being together.

When he reached home he asked around about John Kelly. It seemed she went north to help her sister with her new baby, but she never arrived. Kelly then put two and two together and thought, *"John ran off with her, and just told me he was going to Lynchburg. I heard him talking about California, but how would he have the money to go there. Turner surely wouldn't give Betty any money. Oh well, if he ran off with her, he'll never come back."*

Donald Turner, after sending Cecil to Emma's house, some sixty miles north, found that Betty never arrived. After Cecil reported, Donald thought, *"She's just like her mother and ran off with the first person that came by. To hell with her. I want that land from Lester, and I'll find another way to get it. I'll also find me a wife to do the house chores."*

***

From Ft Smith, they traveled to Ft Worth, Texas. They went to a land office, but the land office didn't know much about the ranchlands of Texas. He suggested that they go to Austin and inquire there. Two weeks later they came to Austin.

The clerk there said, "Most of the land around Austin is taken. My boss said that the governor wants people to go west. He then took out a map, and showed them some of the land west of Marble Falls. That was some sixty miles northwest of Austin.

He said, "That area between Austin and Marble Falls is known as the hill country, because it is mostly hills. I've heard that the land west of Marble Falls has a lot of cattle running wild. It's good ranchland. Some of those people around Marble Falls may be willing to sell. It's pretty far out, and some people just don't have the heart for lonesome livin'.

"You can send us mail if you find a good spot. We've been authorized to sell land at three dollars an acre. Pick you out a place, and let me know if you want to buy the land. Also, let me know if you are buying from someone who owns the land. I'll be able to tell you if the sell is legitimate."

Alton said, "Thanks a lot. You said that there are cattle in that country. Are they free for the taking?"

"I've heard there are lots of cattle, some branded some not branded, but make sure that you aren't horning in on someone who may claim them. They'll hang you as sure as I'm standing here. You see, men of the West are quick to shoot then ask questions."

"Thanks for the tip. I'll take your advice."

After they were driving in the buggy, Louise said, "Maybe we should find something around Austin, it may be safer."

"'Nothing ventured, nothing gained,' as the saying goes. I'll be careful. I plan to have a big ranch, and have four or five boys to help me."

Louise smiled and said, "I'll do my part," and hugged him.

As they drove, Alton said, "We won't do anything in a hurry. We'll look at everything as we go. We might find something close in. However, I want to go further west just to see the country. As I told you before, I want a big ranch. I don't just want enough to sustain us, I want to dwarf my father and your father combined. That's all my dad ever cared about is his land. I feel the same. I guess it's tradition."

They traveled northwest toward Marble Falls. They liked the "Hill Country" as it was called, and particularly liked Marble Falls. They camped there, and began looking around. About the third day Alton was told of a man who was trying to sell a small ranch less than two miles west of town. They drove out to the ranch, and were greeted warmly by Saul

Everett. Saul was about seventy years of age, but his wife was younger.

Saul said, "Get down and come into the house. Effie, we got company." After they were seated, Alton told Saul they was interested in buying his ranch. This brought smiles to both Saul's and Effie's faces.

Saul said, "I'll show you the house while Effie fixes some coffee. After we finish our coffee, I'll take you outside to see the barn and out buildings. Then we'll tour the ranch."

While they were drinking coffee, Saul said, "The ranch is becoming too much for me, and Effie wants to move to town."

"How much land do you have, and how many cattle can you run on what you have?"

"The ranch is about a half section. As a matter of fact it is three hundred and twenty-five acres. I tried to run a hundred and fifty head, but found in a drought, the land will not feed but a hundred, if that. I have divided the land into four pastures and by moving the cattle around, I can keep the cattle feed. Of course in the winter, I have to feed them hay and grain.

"I have forty acres of tillable soil and plant hay and corn. I tried wheat, but that didn't do so good. Corn grows good, as does maize. If you rotate your crops that forty acres will be enough to get you through the winter."

After finishing their coffee, Saul and Alton toured the ranch. Alton noticed Saul only had about thirty head and commented on it.

Saul said, "I sold off most of the cattle, but what you see is good breeding heifers and two good bulls."

When they returned to the house Alton said, "How much do you want for the place?"

"With the house, barn, windmill and tank, I have about two thousand dollars wrapped up in those. I figure the land is worth at least three dollars an acre with the fencing and all.…… Lets say eight thousand dollars. If you want the heifers, they'll cost you twenty dollars each. I'll throw in the two bulls. So that would raise the price by six hundred dollars."

"That is about six thousand more than I have. I have two thousand in cash."

"Well, you could put down the two thousand as a down payment, and I'll take a ten year note for six thousand at two percent interest."

"Would I pay by the month or would you let me sell my beef, and pay for the year at roundup?"

"By the year. I would expect the year's money by the first of November of each year."

"You make it five thousand for the note and throw in the cattle and you'll have yourself a deal."

Saul wanted out. He had waited a year, and no one had the money to buy him out. He studied on it a minute, then said, "How about splitting the difference?"

Alton said, "No, that's about all I could muster for awhile, and even at that, I'm taking a chance. You may get your ranch back, and be two thousand ahead."

Saul's hand went to his chin as he studied and chewed on that awhile.

Effie said, "You've made yourself a deal, Mr. Keller."

Saul smiled and said, "You heard the boss, and put his

hand out and said, "You just bought yourself a ranch, Sonny. Meet me at the bank tomorrow at nine o'clock."

Alton shook his hand and all were smiling. As they were driving back, Louise said, "Where are you going to get seventy cows, Alton?"

"Out west, I guess. We still have enough money to last out the year. After you are set up in the house and everything is running right, I'm off to the West to find cattle."

A frown covered Louise's face and she said, "It could be dangerous alone. Let me go with you. I can ride and help you a lot."

Alton studied on this awhile and said, "You're right, Louise, two is always better than one. We'll get set up, then leave the day after. Has your horse been ridden any?"

"I plan to take the buggy. We can put all our camping gear in it. If I need to ride Patty, I will."

"Sounds like a good plan."

After the business was taken care of, Alton went to the land office and registered his brand as the AK ranch. He then went by the blacksmith and had him forge two branding irons with the AK on the end. They left two days later going west. The second night they camped with an old-timer. As they sat around the campfire, the old timer asked where they were going.

Alton said, "We've heard that there's cattle roaming loose west of here, and that they're free for the taking."

"That may be true, but there's a rancher over near Mason who thinks he owns every cow in Texas. His name is Mason, and his brand is the Bar M. Make sure you don't have any cow with that brand or you'll get your neck stretched. He has about twenty hands who ride for him. He's a greedy man, and even if you don't have any of his cattle, he may still hang you, and keep your herd."

"Thanks for the warning. We'll try to ride shy of him."

The next day they did see some cattle. There were about thirty in a bunch. Alton rode through them and saw two that had the Bar M brand. He cut these out of the herd, and they began to drive the others east.

Alton said, "We'll camp a mile or so from the herd during the day and drive them at night. I'll obliterate our tracks so no one will know where we're camped."

They did this for two nights. Everyday at noon Alton rode carefully to check the herd. The third day he saw a cowboy milling around the herd looking for brands. There were none, of course. After looking carefully, he rode off toward the west.

Alton came back to camp. He said, "I saw a cowboy milling around the herd. He's probably one of Mason's men. He rode off to the west. Let's break camp, and start the cattle east right now. If we drive them the rest of the day, and another night, we may be close to Marble Falls, and they may not follow. Let's go."

Just before morning, a terrific rain storm arrived. They put up the top of their buggy and lowered the side panels and was out of the weather. Let's sleep two hours then drive the cattle due north for about five miles then east again. This may throw them off if they are trailing us. The rain will obliterate the cattle's tracks."

They were dead tired at the end of the day, but they were five or six miles north of the trail they had been following. It was still raining hard. The rider came back with two others.

They couldn't find the herd. They looked for two days, and finally gave up.

When they finally reached their ranch, Alton said, "We need to brand those cattle as soon as possible. I need to get some people to help me."

When they were first riding out to Saul and Effie's place, Alton had notice some Mexican families in shacks at the edge of town.

Alton said, "At the edge of town, I saw several Mexican families. If I have two men, we can have the cattle branded in a day."

The Mexican families were only too glad to get the work, and the branding was done in one day.

About a month later the sheriff of the county came riding out. He saw Alton with his herd and rode over. He said, "I'm checking for unbranded cattle. Old man Mason wants every cow checked. He said that someone took about thirty of his cattle."

"How does he know if they're his if they were unbranded?"

"He says some men road out west and drove about thirty of them east."

"I say again, if they were unbranded how do you know who they belong to?"

"You have a point, but if there are thirty or so unbranded together, he may lay claim to them."

"If you find ten unbranded cows together, I am now laying claim to them. I want you to have them driven to my ranch."

"I can't do that."

"So Mason can and I can't. I wonder what the people of this county will think if you do things for a man that lives outside this county, and won't do them for a citizen of this county."

"Maybe you don't know who Mason is," said the Sheriff.

"Maybe you don't know who I am, Sheriff."

"Who are you?"

"I may be a candidate for county Sheriff next election."

"I get your point. I'll quit checking for Mason's cattle. Who are you anyway?"

"I'm Alton Keller, nephew of an important official in Austin, and I have political ambitions out here."

"Ambitions for what office."

"I'm going to live here awhile before I let that be known. 'Don't be pushed around by anyone.' Those were the last words my uncle said to me."

The sheriff rode off thinking, I had better tell Mason to stay in his own county.

Alton knew he had dodged a bullet. Mason probably had a great deal of influence in this county with the county commissioners. He would have to see about that.

He then began to think about how he could get more cattle. He now had sixty counting the two bulls. Maybe if he went about fifty miles south of where he had taken the unbranded cattle, he would have better luck, and no interference from Mason. He decided to take one of the Mexicans this time. He would tell him he would give him fifty cents for every cow they brought back. Alton was hoping for about fifty head this time.

Cold weather had set in. Saul had left plenty of hay in the barn, but someone had to be at the ranch to feed the stock.

Alton explained this to Louise, and she stayed. She was now pregnant and knew she needed to stay home.

They traveled far to the south, and came to a small town called Blanco. It was on the Blanco River. Alton talked to some old-timers about cattle west of Blanco. He was told that several small ranches ran cattle on the open range. They were always at war with one another. He said, "Make sure the cattle you drive are unbranded."

They traveled down the Blanco River and saw small bunches, some were branded and some weren't. Alton had an idea. He would go about thirty miles further, and then start driving cattle back east. He and Juan would cut out the branded ones. They did this and had fifty or so head when they ran into three ranchers. One of them said, "What do you think you're doing?"

Alton said, "Just doing what Mr. Mason told us to do."

"One of them said, "Oh, we were just asking, good day." After they were away from the men, Juan said, "You are a very smart man, Senor. I think I will join up with you and be your vaquero. I like working for a smart man. Am I hired?"

"You're already hired, Juan. So for, you've made over twenty-five dollars in eight days. I'd say you are making a lot of money."

Juan smiled and said, "I hope we get two thousand cows, I will go to Mexico and be rich."

"All my ranch can handle is a hundred. Once I get that going, I'm going out west and start another ranch. Then I will need two thousand head. I want to give Mason a run for his money."

"Juan said, "I believe you will, Senor Alton. I've hooked my wagon to the right vaquero."

Two years passed and Alton was running a hundred and ten head. He was able to make the payment in November easily by selling his yearlings. He liked to go by Saul's and Effie's house and pay him in cash. Saul always brought out a bottle of brandy and gave him a snort. Effie always hugged and kissed him on the cheek."

Alton said, "The reason I come by and pay you cash is for that kiss Effie always gives me."

Saul said, "You put me on easy street, Alton. How is the farm running?"

"It's doing so good that I'm thinking of going out west to establish a bigger ranch."

"Are you selling the place?"

"No, My wife has two children now. I have a Mexican family that I built a house for, to stay and help Louise. The ranch out west will be a hard life. Right now, she has less than two miles to travel into Marble Falls to get her supplies, and have a little fun. Out west will be hard living. However, Juan and I can get it done. He's a much better cowboy than I am. I'm lucky to have him?"

"What will his wife do?"

"Take care of their four kids. She has her mother to help her."

Alton and Juan left for the West. He told Louise he had no idea when he would return.

CHAPTER 3

THE NEW RANCH

Establishing a new ranch was easy. They homesteaded on a spring that ran into Baron's Creek near Fredericksburg. Alton hired a carpenter, and they built a house and barn, then had a man dig them a well, and put up a tank. The well was a good one and could produce more water than they could ever use.

They were careful and were able to round up over two hundred cows. They branded them, and put them on the open range. That spring they did a round up with several ranches. Mason took the majority of new born calves, but it was split up fairly as Mason had mellowed with age. He was very wealthy, and drove a herd of two thousand steers to market each year.

Alton didn't drive but fifty, and put all his heifers back into his herd. While the other ranchers were warming themselves in the winter. Alton and Juan were finding unbranded cattle and branding them. By the fourth winter his herd was over a thousand. He now had four of Juan's cousins working for him, and built a bunkhouse for them. He had very few disputes as he was more than liberal with his fellow ranchers.

Alton was only home a month are two each year, now. His two boys barely knew him. When he was home he was worried about his herd west of Fredericksburg. He was grumpy a lot of the time, and had little time for his children or Louise.

The youngest son was six now and Louise knew they should be in school. She drove them everyday, then picked they up in the afternoon. She met a woman about her age shopping one day. Her name was Gracie Howard. She was married to Landon Howard, who owned the pharmacy. She found that Gracie lived on the road going to her place. It was the last house going out of town and was only a mile or so from her ranch.

Gracie invited her for lunch, and a strong friendship occurred. Neither had a close friend and both liked one another. After six months, they told their secrets to one another. Louise told how Alton was never home, as he spent at least ten months of the year at there other ranch.

Louise said, "He's changed. Owning all those cattle has made him greedy. He becoming just like his dad. He used to say how greedy his father was and that all he thought about was making his farm bigger and better.

"Alton now wants to be like Tom Mason and own thousands of cattle. I just hope he sees he has enough. I ask him if we could move out to the other ranch, but he said he built a very small house, and it was too crude for a woman and children. I swear he's becoming just like his father. He was the same way."

Actually, he had a housekeeper now, who met all his needs at the ranch. She was a Mexican woman named Ceeley Cordera.

A Change in Tradition

She had lived on four other ranches, but each time before the year was out, she was thrown out by the wife. Ceeley needs were great. Her father moved her each time. He had heard that Senor Keller had a ranch with no woman, so he brought her to Alton and said, "My daughter needs a job, and you are the only person near us who could hire here. Alton hired her, as he hated his own cooking, and the house was always dirty. He had to wash his own clothes, and he never ironed.

Ceeley cleaned his house, and had a delicious meal that night for him. He had not been in bed two minutes until a nude Ceeley was on him.

Alton's needs weren't that great, but Ceeley had him much more than he wanted. No one lived with him in the house as all the \vaqueros were housed in a bunkhouse. Alton found himself staying out on the prairie some nights rather than go home to Ceeley.

She bore him a son the first year. He sent her away to her father after the fifth month, and she didn't return for a year. She did return though, and was at him again. Alton thought, *"That woman knows more about making love than anyone on earth. She can get me anytime she wants, and makes me stay longer that any man would want."*

She bore him another son the next year. Every other year she was gone and always bore him a son. Alton and Ceeley now had four boys, and she was pregnant again. He had to build onto the house. It now had five bedrooms.

He told the men that every time he sent Ceeley away, she came back with a child. As they all had black hair, no one thought that Alton was the father. They all thought that

Alton was a generous man. He paid his men, who were all Mexicans, the same wages white men made, and they were very loyal to him. This had a lot to do because of Juan's loyalty. He had moved Juan's family out to the ranch and built them a house much better than what he and Ceeley lived in. Juan told the men that Senor Keller took care of Ceeley as no one else would.

***

Louise was over at Gracie's for lunch when her husband, Landon, came home. He decided he would have lunch at home, as he had a clerk who could handle the store for an hour or so. He was surprised to see Louise.

Gracie introduced Louise and told him that Louise lived right up the road about a mile and a half. Louise had an instant attraction for Landon and it was mutual. Louise thought to herself that it was just the loneliness of not having a man for so long, that caused the attraction.

As the children were in school Gracie talked Louise into spending the day. They did this several times a week. Landon began coming home nearly everyday for lunch.

That winter Gracie became ill. She became weaker and weaker. Landon had the doctor look at her. The doctor said, "It's just a bad cold." However, she got worse. Landon took her in a buggy to Austin, as he was very worried. Gracie made the trip alright, and was put in a hospital. The doctors in Austin decided she had a lung infection, and began giving her sulfur. This helped her, and she began getting better. She stayed in Austin for nearly two months.

While Gracie was in Austin, Louise came by the pharmacy, and asked about her. Landon said, "She's doing much better, thank you. I miss having lunch with you. I wish I could have a hot lunch, again."

Louise said, "If you want me to, I could go to your house, and fix something for you."

"That would be nice. Please do. It will give me something to look forward to."

Louise put her buggy in the barn in case someone came by and noticed it.

Landon was there right at twelve and Louise had a hot lunch for him. He washed up and then sat down. Louise sat opposite from him. They ate in silence.

When he got up to go, Louise handed him his jacket, and was close to him, so he reached out and brought her to him. He said, "Thank you so much, Louise. She came closer and they kissed. First a small kiss, then it turned into passionate kisses. They both were overcome with passion.

Louise said, "I can't believe what came over me."

"Love is the word, Louise. I know it's wrong. I love Gracie, and I know you do to. However, I want you badly."

Louise said, "Let's think about this overnight. It may sober us up some. I'll meet you tomorrow at noon."

That night she began thinking about their tryst, and was overcome by passion. The next day at noon, she had a lunch for him, and met him at the door. He just took her by the hand and pulled her into the bedroom. They kissed a passionate kiss then were in bed.

Afterward, Landon said, "I have never made love to a

woman so passionate. You do something to me that not even Gracie can do."

"Don't you feel remorse?"

"Yes, but it was beyond wonderful. How do you feel?"

"Like I want you again, and he rolled over on her and they made love again."

They did this every noon for several days then Landon got a letter from Gracie stating she would be home on the one o'clock stage. Landon went home and Louise was about to start lunch. Landon told her about Gracie coming home, and that they should meet her at the stage station.

Gracie was glad to see them. She said, "Please have lunch with us, Louise." Louise nodded and they had lunch.

The next day at lunch Louise was not there, Landon was disappointed, but didn't say so.

Louise began coming by again and visiting. Gracie. Three months later she found she was pregnant. It was a stroke of luck that Alton had been home just after Gracie returned. Louise coached Alton to be with her. They had not had sex for well over a year. She could tell Alton just went through the motions.

However, when she found she was pregnant, she was very glad she had gotten Alton to lie with her. She really had no idea who the father was. Just to be safe, Louise told of an uncle she had in Missouri who looked a lot like Landon. She did this incase the baby was Landon's and looked like him.

Alton was blond with a ruddy completion and Landon had olive skin, with dark hair. When the baby was born he had olive skin and had dark hair. This confirmed that it was

Landon's baby as far as Louise was concerned. She was glad her son was Landon's.

The baby was named Kelton Keller. They all called him Kel. He was five years younger than his closest brother Karl and six years younger that his oldest brother, John Alton Keller, Jr.

Time passed quickly, and now the two older boys were fourteen and fifteen. Alton told Louise that he needed them at the other ranch. She started to protest, but could see it would do no good. Alton had just one thing in mind now, and that was to have the largest ranch in Texas. He was just like what Mason used to be. He established another ranch some seventy miles west of the one he had near Fredericksburg. He came home at Christmas and brought the boys for a week and just after the sell of cattle in the fall. He had since paid off his loan for the Marble Falls ranch.

Kel had been taken by Louise to music lessons after school. He was taught by Gracie. Louise played the piano, but not very good. She bought a piano at the time Kel started his music lessons. Kel was gifted in that area, and by the age of ten was pretty good.

Gracie said, "When he's a teenager, you should take him to Austin to be taught by someone who can teach him much better than me."

***

Kel was about to enter the fifth grade. The school board was meeting and the chair, Doris Singleton, stood which was unusual, so the board knew what she was about to say was important.

She said, "God spoke to me last night. I'm as sure of that as the sun rising. He put in mind that we should teach the Bible to the fifth and sixth graders. They have not reached puberty, and are impressionable at that age. If we could employ some one who could really teach the Bible, it would stick with them their whole life." She then sat down.

Burl Anders, who was often critical of Doris' suggestions, stood and said, "Doris, I sincerely believe God spoke to you. Your words penetrated my heart as if God had spoken those words to me."

Harold Kendal said, "I think we all had the same feeling, Burl. Everyone here knows who that teacher should be."

Lyle Martin had retired from teaching at a seminary, and was now living in Marble Falls on his small pension. He taught a Sunday school class at the Methodist church for men, and now nearly every man in town attended. Lyle had a way of making the characters of the Bible come alive, and gave his message to the men in an interesting way.

Glades Johnson said, "I've never felt so strongly about anything we have done, but I know this was given to us by God Almighty. Not only will the children have a deeper faith, but just think of the historical value. The Bible has more to teach us than any other book that has ever been written. Nearly every book that has been written refers to it in some way. The writer sometimes does not even know that he has employed some of the Bible in his writings, but I think God puts it there.

"We all know the man for this, but we must approach

him in a manor that expresses what has been said tonight. Thank you Doris for your close walk with our Lord. I shall never forget this night, and I'm sure none of you won't. I think we should give Lyle a good salary, maybe not as much as a full time teacher, but substantial enough to compensate him nicely."

So it was set. The school board along with the superintendent went to Martin. Doris explained what she had told the board about God speaking to her."

Lyle, smiled and said, "If God has ordained it, how could I refuse." Thus started the Bible classes for the fifth and sixth grades at Marble Falls.

As Kel was starting the fifth grade, he was impressed with Professor Martin's teaching. He would study the Bible as much as he did anything.

One man stood in church and said, "Before our son began the Bible class that Professor Martin teaches at the school, I could barely get Arthur to do his homework. Now he can't wait to get home to look up and study what the Professor taught them.

Another woman told her Sunday school class. My husband rarely says anything about religion, but after our Wanda had us read a chapter of the proverbs each morning, it impressed my husband so greatly, that he prayed the first day after Wanda read the chapter praising the Lord for opening his eyes. He said such sweet things, I cried like a baby. Our family has surely changed. We now talk about the stories that the Professor teaches Wanda."

Another woman said, "He's changed all our lives. My, the school board surely did the right thing."

The class made a deep impression on Kel. Louise could see that it had. She spoke to Gracie about Kel. She knew that Kel was as much her boy as hers. Gracie said, "I read a book by D. L. Moody, the great evangelist. I found that they print his sermons. Let's send for them. For a small fee they will send us a copy each week that we can share with our boy."

Louise loved it when Gracie referred to Kel as part hers. They did send away for the sermons, and Kel read and discussed them with both Louise and Gracie. It made a great impression on Kel.

When Kel was entering high school, the school board was at their meeting and Doris again stood. When she did this, all knew that what she was about to tell them was profound, as she had not stood since she revealed to them what God had given her about teaching the Bible.

Doris said, "I was reading a book that said, Greek and Latin are the foundation of every language. We should be teaching them here. Gordon Elders lives in Marble Falls and he used to teach both subjects at the college in Austin. I think our children could receive something that would edify their lives. What do you people think?"

Burl Anders said, "Again, Doris you have been given a revelation that will educate our children like we all want. I for one am for it."

The rest agreed and Gordon Elders was persuaded to teach the class. The board had decided to make the courses electives so students could either take them or not. Kel was the first to sign up. He was Mr. Elder's prize student as Louise and Gracie both helped him and they learned, also.

However, at age thirteen, Alton told Louise he was taking

Kel to the ranch as he was needed. This time Louise protested. Alton insisted. She told him if he took Kel, she would divorce him, and sue for custody of all the children.

This shocked Alton. He never thought that Louise would leave him. He relented then, and Kel stayed with Louise.

Kel's teachers could see he was much smarter than the other students. He had a thirst for knowledge, and Louise and Gracie did everything they could to encourage him.

Three years later he graduated from high school. He was now seventeen.

Alton then took him to the ranch west of Fredericksburg. Kel went willingly as he thought learning to be cowboy may help him understand his father. He saw Alton as a greedy man with only one goal in life, and that was to have the most cattle in Texas.

That winter Gracie had her lung problem reoccur. She had only had it a week, but Landon took her to Austin immediately. They prescribed a sulfur treatment again and she came home with Landon. She was still sick, so Landon asked Louise to stay with Gracie during the day.

Gracie had a premonition that she may die. She said, "Louise, I may not make it this time. I want you to promise me you will tend to Landon. I know he loves you, and I expect you love him, also. I finally figured out why Kel looks like Landon. It's because he is his father. I'm glad he's his father. I'm glad that you were there for Landon. I was never jealous or resented it. I understand those things. I remembered the first time you met. When your eyes came together, there were nearly sparks in the air. I was happy for you both. I had a feeling I would die early, and I wanted you to love each other.

I knew Landon loved me. He loves us both. Be good to him, Louise, and give him more children if you can."

Louise was crying now and Gracie put her hand over, and brought Louise to her. She said, "I have never had a friend I loved like you, Louise. You made my life so much richer."

Gracie passed away a week later. It was a hard time for both Landon and Louise.

When they were alone Landon said, "I'm putting the store up for sale. I'm going to take a job in Austin. I have been asked every year by a man in his seventies, who I have known since childhood. He's the reason I became a pharmacist. He wants me to be his partner. He has no children, and I think he wants to pass the store on to me when he dies.

"I'll stay there six months. Then you write a note to Alton and tell him you are going home. Say you may be back or maybe not. However, you come to me in Austin. I will have a nice house for you by that time. I will have all of my furniture sent to Austin after I sell the house here You will come won't you?"

"Of course, I promised Gracie. She told me she knew all about us and that Kel was your son. She was happy for Kel, because she could not give you children. She said she was very happy that we loved each other. Did you know she stayed in Austin another two weeks, so we would be together? You had the sweetest wife in the world, Landon."

Landon was crying and said, "I loved her so much. I had no idea that she wanted us together."

It all went as Landon planned it. Louise left a note for Alton. She signed it Betty.

Alton took stock of his life then. He saw where he had just cut Louise out of his life. He knew he could never get her back, now. It was too late. He resigned himself to Ceeley. He loved her now and she more than loved Alton. She fit Alton much better than Louise and had given him seven boys and not one girl. Ceeley still made love to him every night he was home.

CHAPTER 4

RANCH LIFE FOR KEL

Kel was sent to the most western ranch. Kel met a man at the ranch the first day he arrived. The man's name was Darvin Sykes. Darvin was in his early forties. He had been a cowboy all his life. He had never married and loved the cowboy life. As they arrived the same day, Darvin asked Kel to be his partner. Kel knew every cowboy had a partner, and he was flattered a man in his forties would choose him. Darvin had no idea that Kel was the boss' son, and Kel surely didn't want anyone to know.

Kel learned a lot each day from Darvin and Darvin enjoyed teaching such a willing student. They all wore side arms. Darvin asked Kel if he had ever fired his pistol and Kel said, "No, my mother was too busy giving me piano lessons."

This sent Darvin into a fit of laughter. He said, "Kel, I chose the right partner. You keep me laughing all day long. I've had several partners in my life, but you are the best I ever had. I hope you will stick with me all my life. It's just a joy to be around you.

"Anyway getting back to the pistol, I'm going to teach you

so you will be as good as the rest of the hard cases you may run up against."

Every chance they got, Darvin would instruct Kel. Kel had quick hands. He attributed this to the piano as he could run scales faster than Gracie had ever seen anyone do. Darvin was amazed how good Kel was with a pistol. He had impressed on Kel the importance of hitting what he shot at. He said, "It doesn't matter how fast you are, if you don't hit your target.

"I hope you never have to face a man, but if you do, it's much different than shooting at a target. Immediately, think of the man as a target, forget he's a man, he's just your target. If you can get this through your mind, you have won ninety percent of the battle. The other ten percent is hitting your target. Some men will try to talk you as they know if you are sweating, you won't be much good. When they do that just think, '*You're only a target, so get on with it.*'"

They never went into town as Darvin knew Kel was too young to drink. When they had some time off, which was little, they either went hunting or fishing.

However, one Saturday the foreman sent them to the railroad station near San Antonio to pick up a load of barbed wire. Darvin wanted a drink. There was a bar where several horses were tied out front. They entered the bar and Darvin ordered his drink. The bartender looked at Kel and Kel just moved his head back and forth indicating he didn't want anything.

A man next to him said, "When a man speaks to you, answer him!"

Darvin said, "Are you this boy's father?"

The man said, "No."

"Then shut up, and mind your own damn business."

The man said, "Hey, aren't you one of those Keller riders?"

Kel pulled away from the bar and said, "He said, shut up, and that's what he meant."

"Oh, this young squirt needs a spanking."

Kel said, "I'm about to kill you, and you're talking of spanking?"

The man saw Kel in a different light, now. He had heard of young killers. He said, "Forget it kid. Just forget it."

Kel said, "Good enough."

When they left the bar, Darvin said, "You could have gotten us killed back there."

"No, I could tell he was all bluff. I don't know how I know, but I know."

Darvin thought awhile and said, "Yes, I think you do. You've told me how cows are going to move, and they always go just like you say. You have a gift, Kel. I've heard of that. However, what would you have done if he had drawn on you?"

"He would have been a target."

Darvin laughed again. "Damn it, Kel, at least once a week, you say things that is so funny, I nearly choke. What a pleasure it is to ride with you. I bet ole man Keller would take you with him, if he knew how funny you were. By the way what does Kel stand for?"

"Kelton. My ma named me that."

"Where is your ma?"

"Back in Marble Falls waiting for me to write. I write once a week, but she would like me to write everyday. I have two older brothers that work out of the Fredericksburg ranch. They never write, but she doesn't ask them."

"My gosh, how many ranches does the boss own?"

"Three that I'm aware of. There is never enough for him."

"Yeah, I've heard of men like that. However, you and I will never be like that."

"I can promise you I won't. I have life by the tail, I get to ride with Darvin Styles."

Davin again laughed and said, "Now don't set your sights too high, Kel?" and this time Kel laughed. He said, "Darvin, I've got the right partner."

They were chasing some cows out of the breaks when four cowboys rode up. One of them said, "Those are Mason's cows."

Darvin said, "If you'll look closely, that one with the white spot on it's rear shows the AK brand."

"I don't give a shit what brand is on it, I said those are Mason's cows."

Kel said, "I'll bet your life that they're AK cows."

The cowboy's eye's narrowed and said, "Are you calling me a liar?"

"No, I'm calling you someone who is trying to take AK cows."

"With that the man's hand went down to his gun, but before he pulled it completely out, he was dead. Kel put his gun away and said, "Any others?" It happened so fast that everyone was in astonishment.

One of the cowboys said, "Our friend was mistaken. We'll take him, and leave."

Word got quickly to Alton about the shooting. He was there the next day. He called Darvin and Kel in and said, "A Mason man was killed yesterday by you two."

"No," Kel said. "Darvin had nothing to do with it. The man tried to take our cattle, and when I called him on it, he drew on me and I shot him."

Alton said, "Couldn't you have just wounded him?"

Kel used Darvin's words and said, "When a man draws his gun on you, he means to kill you, not wound you. I did what I had to do."

"Well, we're in serious trouble now. Mason may make war on us."

"Why don't I go over and see Mason and explain it to him."

"He'll shoot you dead or hang you, Son."

"No, I'll explain it clearly, and have the men who were with the man I shot, come in and tell what they saw. Most cowboys are honest men, and would not lie, no matter what."

"I see your point. I don't think he will shoot a kid."

Darvin said, "I'll go with him."

Kel said, "No, Darvin, it will be safer if I go alone, unarmed. I can truthfully say that I was not sent by you, Boss."

"I think you're right Kel. It may save a range war where many people's lives would be lost."

Alton left. The next morning Kel took a bath and put on his best clothes. He rode slowly so he would get there when the hands had called it a day. After four that afternoon, he was riding in under the Mason arched gate.

Many people looked at him, but none stopped him. He rode up to the ranch house that was a mansion. He tied his horse out front and walked up to the door. A maid opened the door.

Kel said, "I'm here to see Mr. Mason about a private

matter. The maid left, then returned and said, "He will see you now. Kel came in and Mason shook his hand. He said, Are you looking for work young man?"

"No Sir, I'm here to talk to you about the shooting day before yesterday."

The smile left Mason's face. He was shocked. He said, "That's a serious matter, Son. Why are you here?"

"First of all, I was not sent by Mr. Keller, I came on my own volition to explain what happened. Can you call in the men who were at the shooting? It will help me to explain." Mandy, go fetch Jimmy, Wheeler and Billy Bob. Will you have some water, Son?"

"No Sir, I'm fine."

"In just a few minutes the men came in. They had just ridden up and were dusty and sweaty. They did not recognize Kel as he had take off his hat when he entered the house, and he was wearing a white shirt and some nice pants.

Mason said, "This young man is here to explain the shooting of Max. Proceed son."

Kel said, "Like I said, I was not sent by Mr. Keller, I came on my own volition. I was the one who did the shooting. I would ask you men to tell exactly what happened.

Jimmy said, "Max, he told two riders of the AK that the cows they were chasing out of the brakes were Mason cows. The man with this kid said that one of the cows had the AK brand on it, which it did. Max wouldn't let well enough alone, as anyone could see that one of them had the AK brand."

Max said, "'I don't give a shit whose brand is on that cow, these are Mason cows.'"

The kid said, 'I'll bet your life that you're wrong.' Then Max said, 'Are you calling me a liar?'"

And the kid said, "No, I'm saying you are trying to take AK cattle.' That's when Max went for his gun. The kid was lightning fast, and killed Max as he drew his gun. That's as clear as I saw it, maybe the others saw it differently."

Mason looked at both men and they both nodded as if to say that was what was what they saw and heard.

Mason set back and said, "Can you see you helped provoke the fight, Son."

"Yes Sir, I feel terrible about it. I came so you could decide what to do with me. Mr. Keller and his men had nothing to do with this, and I'm here to prevent any retaliation. My partner said, you would probably hang me. But I'm here to let you decide and not to get anyone else killed."

"You are a brave man, Son. I respect you for coming in. What do you fellows think? You were there."

Wheeler said, "It surely didn't have to come to a killing. Max was wrong, and he pulled on the kid, here. I think the kid provoked him some, and is not altogether innocent, but he didn't draw first."

"Billy Bob."

Wheeler told it right. I myself admire this boy for coming in and telling it straight out."

Mason said, "How much do you make, Son?"

"Thirty a month and found."

"Max has a mother in Junction. I think you should take her a hundred and eighty dollars, that's half a years pay. Also, take all his belongings to her. Don't tell her you killed her boy. It would just hurt her more. Just tell her you were sent to bring all of his belongings. Will you do that?"

"Yes Sir. I can come by here next Friday and take it to her. I have some savings that I can use. I feel terrible about what I did. If I had it to do over, I would have let Max have the cows. People may think I'm a coward, but I will back down from any fight from, now on."

Billy Bob said, "I think that is the thing to do. No one could out draw you and you know it, so it would be murder if you drew your gun."

Kel said, "Thank you Billy Bob, that is sound advise and I will follow it."

Kel left and after he had gone Mason said, "I wish he were my boy."

Wheeler said, "I do, too. A finer boy never walked this earth. Can you image the guts it took to have come here to Mr. Mason, knowing he could be hung?"

Billy Bob said, "I think he would have never said a word if you said you were going to hang him, Boss. He felt so badly, he wanted some punishment. I think you done the right thing having him go to Max's mother to tell her. I just hope this doesn't break his spirit."

Mason said, "No, he's got too much backbone. I would like to see what becomes of him. Did anyone get his last name?" All three shook their heads.

"I think I will write Keller a letter telling all that went on today. I will say that he has one hell of a cowboy working for him. I will also say I wish he were my son."

When Alton got the letter he read it three times with great pride. However, when he dropped by the western ranch, Kel was not there. The foreman said, "Kel said he was riding into Junction to take some belongings to a man's mother. He drew his wages and said he wouldn't be back."

Darvin was there and said, "He told me goodbye and thanked me. For what I don't know. I taught him to shoot, but the kid has natural talent. I wish I hadn't taught him to shoot. He's too damn good at it. I just hope no one else ever draws on Kel, because they will be dead if they do. I wonder who his folks were?"

Alton said, "He's my son." Darvin was shocked.

"He never said a thing about being the boss' son."

"He wouldn't. That's just Kel. I wonder if I will ever see him again?" Alton asked rhetorically as everyone looked at Alton.

After Alton left Darvin said, "If Kel were my son, I could never quit bragging about him. He's the best man I ever knew, and he's just a kid."

CHAPTER 5

A DEPUTY SHERIFF

In Junction Kel found Max's mother at her home. He told her Max had had a fatal accident. He said, "Max was a top hand and was well liked. His last words were about you, Ma'am. He asked me to take his belongings and this money to you. It was all he had, but he wanted you to have it."

His mother had tears in her eyes and said, "Ranch life must have changed him. He was a hard one to raise. I thought eventually someone would kill him. He said outrages things to people. I was constantly called down to the school for his bad behavior. You can't know how it comforts me to know he became a good person. I think being a cowboy helped him grow out of his bad behavior as a youth. Thanks so much for coming and telling me."

After Kel left, Max's mother thought, *"I didn't even ask that young man's name."*

Kel rode into San Antonio. He was looking for a job. He was through being a cowboy. He wanted an education, and heard they had a college in San Antonio. He stopped to get something to eat as it was about noon when he arrived. There was a newspaper left on the table where he was sitting. It was folded so the want ads were facing him. As he was waiting for the waiter, he began to read the help wanted ads. He saw where the sheriff needed a night jailor. Nothing else was said in the ad, but Kel began to think. *"If I could be a night jailor, I would have time to go to college during the daytime."*

After eating, he asked the waiter where the sheriff's office was located. The waiter gave him directions. At the sheriff's office, Kel asked a deputy if he could talk to the sheriff? A voice from another desk said, "I'm the sheriff."

Kel said, "I read where you were looking for a night jailor. I'm here to apply for the job."

The sheriff said, "How old are you, Son?"

Kel lied and said twenty-two, Sir."

The sheriff shook his head and said, "Every year the kids look younger, Harold. The night jailor's job is still open, if you want it. It pays thirty a month. You're on duty from six in the afternoon until six in the morning. That's when Harold comes on duty. If something happens where nobody shows up, you stay here until someone does.

"You work every night and can take off when the cells are empty, which is seldom, but it does happen. If you don't have a place to stay, you can use an empty cell for a week or two, until you can find some place. Believe me, after you spend sometime using the cell as a home, you'll want your own place. I want you to be on the job with Harold here, so he can break you in. Listen to him, he will save you a lot of grief and maybe your life. What's your name, Son?"

"John Kelly, Sir, but my friends call me Kel."

"Fill out this form, Kelly, then take it over to the courthouse after I sign it, and give it to the County Treasure. He writes the checks so you can get paid each month. I'll expect you here at five o'clock tonight, so Harold can brief you. Now let me say this again. Listen to Harold. He's been here twenty years and is still alive. The prisoners are all con men. Never listen to them unless they say they're sick. Then go get another deputy. Never enter a cell. If a doctor is needed, keep a gun on the prisoner the whole time the doctor is in there. If the prisoner makes a wrong move, shoot him. Have you ever shot someone?"

"Yes Sir?"

"Did you kill him?"

"Yes Sir."

"Tell me about it.'

"He just told the part about the fight and how Max drew on him."

"Are you good with a gun?"

"Pretty good, but I never want to use it if there is anyway, other than dying."

"I like your attitude. If I have an opening for a deputy, I'll put you on as a regular deputy. That job pays fifty a month, but you have to wear a badge. The county will pay you twenty dollars a year for clothing allowance."

That very night Deputy Sloan was shot. He wasn't killed, but was wounded seriously. Kel was in a jail cell when the sheriff came in and woke him up. He said, "Kelly, I need a man with me. There has been some trouble, and I need you to go with me to the Palace Saloon. Here, strap on his gun."

"I have my own that I'm used to."

"Here's a badge walk behind me, and cover me if trouble starts."

47

"They went into the bar, and four cowboys were standing at the bar. One of them said, "I thought you'd drop by, Sheriff. Your deputy tried to take our guns away and couldn't. Are you going to try?"

Before he could answer Kel drew, and shot the gun out of the hand of a man at the end of the bar who had brandished it.

The sheriff said, there's your answer. Do you want to drop your gun belts or do I take them off your corpses."

The men were awed at the speed of Kel's gun, and how he shot the gun instead of the man. They all dropped their gun belts. Kel picked them up, and the gun he had shot from the man's hand. He then followed the sheriff as he marched the men to jail.

When they were in their cells, the sheriff told his prisoners, "You are under arrest for attempted murder and if Shelby dies, you will probably hang." It was quiet as a tomb when they left.

When they were back in the office, the sheriff turned to Kel and said, "That was a damn fool thing you did, shooting the gun instead of the man. If you had missed, I might have been killed."

Kel said, "And if I hadn't have seen that guy hidden around the bar you might have been dead. I know my capabilities, Sheriff. I hit what I shoot at."

After that arrest, the sheriff made him a deputy. Kel had to be sworn in by the judge over in the courthouse. He also dropped off the form to the county treasurer so that he would get paid as a deputy sheriff.

The treasurer smiled and said, "Promoted the next day, I guess you'll be the sheriff by the end of the week."

Kel was good at his job. He solved a case where some

cattle had been stolen from a feeding lot. He had noticed another pen on the other end of town. He examined the brand carefully. He went and got the sheriff and another deputy. When the sheriff arrived, Kel shot one of the steers dead in front of the sheriff. The sheriff was appalled until Kel took his knife and skinned the hide around the new brand. On the backside you could see that the steer had been re-branded.

The sheriff said, "What if you had been wrong, Kel?"

"I've worked cattle enough to know a running iron had been used on this steer and several others."

The owner came out. He had been down the street, but heard the shot. When he saw the sheriff, he came up and said, "Who shot my steer?"

"It's not your steer, Elmer, we shot the steer and skinned the hide to look at the brand."

"How did you know to do that."

"Deputy Kelly is an expert on cattle rustling. He killed a man just a few months ago for doing this very thing."

Elmer began to back up then, as he looked at Kel who was now staring at him. The sheriff said, "He's not going to shoot you, Elmer. Just tell us how you came by these cattle."

Elmer began to stutter then said, "Two men brought them to me and offered them to me for fifteen dollars a head. I couldn't pass up an offer like that."

Kel said, "The brands must have been fresh. Didn't you think that a running iron had been used?" "I could see the brands were fresh, but they said that they were unbranded when they found them."

The sheriff then said, "Elmer, you know there are no

unbranded cows around here. The ranches have taken all the unbranded steers their age. Didn't you question that?"

"I guess I was too greedy."

"I guess you were. Now you have to drive the cattle back to the railroad holding pens and take the loss. I want you also to pay the company for that dead steer. You can butcher it and probably sell the meat to the Slim at his meat market."

Elmer's head was now down and he mumbled, "Okay, I'll do it first thing in the morning."

As they walked away the sheriff said, "Do you believe his story, Kel?"

"It doesn't matter. He probably won't do it again. He will just keep doing his job and paying taxes instead of costing the state for his stay at Huntsville."

The sheriff said, "You are better than any of my deputies. None of them could have solved that crime. I have a dozy of a crime for you. It is a series of missing people. I assume they are dead, but you never know.

"Let's go to Hazel's café and I'll tell you about it. Then you can go over all the missing persons forms, and see if they are connected. I have puzzled over them for a couple of years now."

CHAPTER 6
THE TREE WIDOW

Henry and Tilly Mathews lived south of San Antonio. They ran just enough cattle to sustain them. Henry was a big fellow about six-four and weighed about two-fifty. Tilly was not much smaller. She was over six feet and easily weighed two-thirty.

They had a son, Billy, who was bigger than both his parents. He was six-six and weighed about two-fifty. He was as strong as a bull. However, Billy never progressed past the age of six, mentally. He obeyed everything Tilly asked him to do. She was devoted to him.

Henry didn't dote on him. He made him work hard, and sometimes beat him, but never around Tilly. She loved the boy. He was now in his late teens. He always had a smile on his face, and went with Tilly to town to shop. She would always buy him candy. The boy loved his mother.

Henry inherited twenty-four thousand dollars from the sale of all his uncles businesses in Dallas. Henry had no idea his uncle owned that much property. When the money came, he put it in the bank. He told Tilly about the bonanza, and showed her the bank statement. He had kept a thousand dollars cash so they could spend some of the money.

Henry began to keep whiskey around the house now. He drank a good deal of the time and became angry when he drank. He started beating Billy, and this set Tilly into a rage. She had knockout drops they had used to trap coyotes that raided their chickens.

One day Henry put Billy to mow hay in the barn. He told him how to stack the bales, but Billy got it wrong, and all the hay had to come back out and be mowed again. Henry had been drinking, and was mad over the mistake. He made Billy restack the hay and then beat him with a rein until he cut him on his back. Billy just took it, but Tilly was madder than she had ever been.

Billy always went to bed when the sun went down. After Billy was asleep, Tilly made some coffee, and told Henry she wanted him to get a churn from the barn. Henry drank his coffee, then walked out to the barn. He collapsed in the barn as Tilly had laced his coffee with the knockout drops. She had followed Henry to the barn. She saddled a horse, then took a rope and threw it over a rafter. After making a noose around Henry's head, she hooked the other end of the rope around the saddle horn and walked the horse off until Henry's feet were about two feet off the ground. He quit breathing, and died.

After tying the rope off, she took a stool that was about two and a half feet off the ground and put it where Henry hung.

The next morning she took Billy with her and drove to town. She went to Sheriff Wilson and told him that Henry had hung himself. Wilson got Bill Owens, the local undertaker, to drive his wagon with them. When they got to the house she told Billy to go in and wait for her.

They cut down Henry and took him to town. They buried Henry in the local cemetery, and conducted a graveside service the next day. Henry was in a wooden casket so Billy was unaware of what they were doing. That night he asked about Henry. Tilly told him that Henry had to leave for the army. Tilly had read Billy several books about the army, so he took it as a natural thing.

Tilly belonged to a quilting club. Several women would get together once a week at the church and quilt. It was a place to pass around gossip which they all enjoyed. Tilly had a friend named Rachel Holman. Her husband, Derrick, was a blacksmith, and good at his trade. He had a thriving business and employed two other blacksmiths to help him.

Derrick was frugal with his money, and had accumulated quite a sum. He had one flaw. When he drank he became angry. He would sometime beat Rachel. Once at the quilting party, Rachel came in with black eyes and a swollen face. This riled Tilly. No one said anything to Rachel and acted like she was normal. This happened about three times a year.

About a year after Henry had been hung, Rachel again was at the quilting bruised up. Tilly called on her right after the quilting. Rachel invited her in, and they talked. Tilly told how Henry had beaten Billy, sometimes very badly. She then said, "But I ended it."

Rachel's eyes grew as she understood the implication. Tilly then said, "Would you like me to end your beatings?"

Rachel said, "They are getting more sever and more often, now. I think he will eventually kill me."

"If you say it's okay, I will make him disappear. You won't know anything about it, but he will just disappear."

"That sounds like something I would like. I could then have mother move here. She needs me badly, but Derrick won't let her move in. How will you do it?"

"You don't want to know. I just wanted your permission."

"Have at it. The sooner the better."

On her way home, Tilly stopped by the smithy and had Derrick come over to look at a shoe on her horse. When he arrived, Tilly said, "Derrick, I have a pearl handled revolver that Henry owned. He always liked you. I want you to have it. Now it would look strange you coming out to see me, as I'm a widow and all, so don't tell a soul, not even Rachel. Ride out to my place tonight about nine o'clock. No one will see you then. Will you come?"

"Sure, Tilly. I'll make sure no one knows I came to see you. I will see you at nine tonight."

Tilly had Billy dig a three foot in diameter hole for Tilly's tree two days prior. Tilly had Billy dig it eight feet deep She helped him haul out the dirt with a bucket and put a ladder down for him. She put a wagon wheel over the hole, so no one would fall in, as Billy sometimes didn't look where he was going.

That night Billy was asleep when Derrick rode up. Tilly had put the dogs in the barn and met Derrick at the porch. She said, "Be real quiet, Billy's asleep. They went in and the pistol was laying on the kitchen table. Tilly said, "Would you have a cup of coffee with me?"

Derrick said, "That would be nice, Tilly. He was now handling the gun. Tilly poured him a cup and watched him drink it. After awhile he slumped in his chair, passed out. She first took his wallet and removed all the money in it. She then put his wallet back and dragged him outside. She removed the wagon wheel, and pushed Derrick into the hole. She went to his horse and stripped it, then threw the saddle and gear down into the hole. As she put the dirt back in the hole she added water so the dirt will fill every niche and cranny. She filled the hole three quarters full and tamped it down until it was solid. She saddled her horse and led Derricks horse away.

She traveled to the Tobin farm about five miles away. She knew that Tobin had a group of horses in his north pasture. She removed the bridle of Derricks horse and let him mingle with the rest of the horses. She returned that night and went to bed. The next morning after breakfast she went with Billy and finished covering the hole. She used a lot of water to make sure the soil in the hole packed around the body and saddle. She then planted a poplar tree in the hole.

When Derrick didn't show up at the smithy, one of the men came to Rachel and asked if Derrick was ill. Rachel said, "He never came home last night. He told me he had an errand to run, and left a little after eight o'clock, but never returned. I've been crazy with worry."

The man said, "I'll go get Sheriff Wilson. Wilson came to the house, but Rachel had no information. A week went by, then three weeks went by. Tobin came to town one day with Derricks horse.

He told how he didn't know when Derrick's horse was put with his horses. "I noticed the horse this morning as I

55

was giving them some hay. I have no idea how long he's been there."

Wilson said, "Well, we now know he didn't just ride off. Someone must have done him in. Don't tell anyone about this as it would just upset Rachel. Her mother is coming this week as she needs the company."

Wilson had a sharp deputy working with him, named. Reilly Andrews. They were talking one day about Derricks disappearance. Reilly said, "You know, I've been checking around about Henry Mathews. Everyone I talked with said he wasn't the type to kill himself. He might kill someone else, but they were amazed he hung himself. Maybe there's a connection between Derrick's disappearance and Henry hanging himself."

"That's pretty far out there Reilly, but have at it. It's your case, now."

Reilly said, I'm going to check some other things, I'll tell you about it later. I may not go out to the Mathew place for awhile."

However, Reilly changed his mind. After he talked to Mrs. Holman, asking her if she had remembered anything else. He then said, "Was Henry Mathews and your husband friends?"

This alarmed Rachel although she tried not to show it. However, Reilly noticed her eyes grow large with the question. It was subtle, but it was there. It was getting late, but he decided to talk to Tilly and see if she showed any alarm with the question.

He took a short cut and bypassed the town. When he arrived, Tilly met him at the the front gate as the dogs were barking wildly. She said, "Give me a minute and I'll put up the dogs."

She said, "It's late, how come you came out here so late, deputy? Come on in. They sat at the kitchen table and he asked Tilly if her husband and Mr. Holman were friends. He could tell it unnerved her although she masked it pretty well.

She said, "They were friends, but not close friends."

"As close as you and Mrs. Holman?"

"No."

"I understand you and Mrs. Holman were close friends. One of the ladies at the quilting party told me you were very upset when Rachel would come in showing the marks of her husband's beatings."

Tilly could tell the deputy was onto something. She thought if Rachel were subjected to questioning severely, she might just break. She then said, "Would you like a cup of coffee, deputy?"

"Why yes, that would be nice of you."

The deputies back was turned away from the stove and cupboards. Tilly laced his coffee with the knockout drops and said, "Are you the only one working on the Holman case, deputy?"

"Yes, the sheriff gave it to me, because he was getting no where."

Tilly served him the coffee, and in just a few minutes he slumped in his chair. Billy was in bed and she tucked him in and kissed him goodnight. She then quietly dragged the Deputy out to a hole Billy had finished that day for another poplar tree. She took all his money then dumped him into the hole. She went and stripped his horse and put that in the hole. She spent an hour covering up the hole, then saddled up, and pulled the deputies horse with her. She had heard Holman's horse had been found at Tobin's farm, so she went the opposite direction with Reilly's horse. She traveled about five miles then took the halter off and let him go. The horse kept traveling in the same direction. She watched him go, then turned around and went home. The next morning she saturated the dirt in the hole with water to pack it down, and Billy completed filling the hole, then she planted another poplar tree.

When Reilly didn't show up to work the next day, Sheriff Wilson went to his house. He wasn't married now, as his wife had gone home to her mother. He had been seeing a young widow and Wilson asked if she had seen him. Of course she hadn't.

Wilson knew that Reilly was going to see Mrs. Holman, so he talked to her. She said, "Yes, he asked just a few questions then left. That's all I know."

Wilson rubbed his chin and was completely baffled. He found a letter in Reilly's apartment from his wife saying she was divorcing him The letter asked him to sign the papers she sent. Wilson couldn't find the papers, so he assumed he sent them. The letter was three months old.

Wilson then wrote to Andrew's wife asking if he had been to see her. Two weeks later she replied, and said he hadn't.

***

When the sheriff and Kel returned to the office the sheriff began to tell the story. He said, "About four years ago Tilly

Mathews came to my office and told me her husband had hung himself. I got Bill Owens to follow us out with his hearse. Sure enough, old Henry was swinging in the barn. We cut him down and Bill put him in his hearse and took him to town. I stayed there to ask Tilly a few question.

"Henry was not very sociable, but I never thought he would kill himself. However, having to be married to Tilly would make me think about it. They had this one child who is touched in the head. His name is Billy. Billy has the mind of a six or seven year old. Guess he was born that way. He loves Tilly though, and she dotes on him. She used to drive to town to get her supplies and Billy would come with her. Now, though, Billy comes in the wagon alone, and hands Mel Belter the list Tilly gives him, and they load it, then Billy drives home.

"Tilly has but one event, other than church, that she attends, and that's the quilting society. About twelve women get together and pass all the gossip around, while they work on a quilt. Tilly has a friend in that group that she now visits, but she never used to visit her, because of her husband. Their names are Derrick and Rachel Holman. Derrick was a big surly man. I say 'was,' as he disappeared nearly two years ago.

"Derrick, often as not, would beat Rachel. I understand that Rachel would come to the quilting party, and would have black eyes and whelps on her.

"About a year and a half ago, Holman didn't show up to his smithy, where he was a blacksmith. No one has seen him since. He wasn't the type that would just up and leave a good business. So that's a mystery. His horse was found with

Tobin's horses about two weeks later, with no saddle or bridal. So I think someone did him in."

"Do you think there's a connection between Tilly's husband hanging himself and Holman disappearing?" Kel asked.

"I don't know. That is something I was hoping you would find out. I put Reilly Andrews, my deputy, on the case. He told me he was going to interview Rachel Holman and a few others around town. That was six months ago.

"Andrews never came back to the office, he just disappeared. I interviewed Mrs. Holman and she confirmed that Reilly visited her, but only asked a few questions about her husband's disappearance, then rode away. The next day I went out with Harold to the Mathew's farm. Tilly met us at the gate. Her dogs were barking fiercely so she had to chain them up. I asked her about Reilly and she said he never came out to her place.

"We found his horse a few days later mixed in with some farmer's horses. It was in the opposite direction of Tobin's farm, but again their was no trace of his saddle or things on it. The disappearances of two men made me think that all of these were connected. I have no evidence that they were, it's just a feeling.

"Tilly is a big woman. She's six feet at least, and weighs over two hundred pounds. That son of hers is about six-six and weighs at least two-fifty. However, I don't think Tilly or Billy could overpower Reilly. Reilly was smart and wouldn't let Tilly get him into a position that he couldn't get out of.

"Well, you have what I know. I think a different set of eyes will see more than I did. Three men have died and I think Tilly had something to do with all of them."

"How does Tilly and Billy make a living?"

"Oh, I left out a vital piece of evidence. Henry's uncle died about six months before he did. He inherited twenty-four thousand dollars from him. Tilly ended up with the money. She took five thousand in cash, and left the rest in a savings account. She pays cash for everything. I think it's enough to last she and Billy a long time.

"How does Rachel Holman make a living?"

"She sold her husband's smithy, and he had a substantial amount of savings. She inherited all of it after a year, so she has enough to last her."

"Thanks sheriff. I think I'll start with Rachel and see how that goes."

***

At Rachel's house Kel was cordially invited in and offered a cup of coffee. Harold had warmed Kel to never take anything from anyone who was associated with a crime as it could be poisoned. He thought of Harold's warning and said, "No thank you, Ma'am. I'm just here to ask you a few questions about your husband's disappearance. Rachal's expression changed to fright. This told Kel she may know something of how he disappeared.

Kel said, "Why do you think your husband disappeared?"

With big eyes she said, "I have no idea. He was here and then he was gone. I thought he may have left with a woman."

"Had you or anyone else ever see him with another woman?"

"Well, no."

"If he left town he would surely take some of his money with him, but not a cent left the bank, I'm told. That tells me that someone must have done him in. I asked around to see if anyone had had a dispute with him. No one said anything about a dispute. They all said he didn't have a warm disposition, but everyone said he was never rude to anyone.

"I understand he abused you several times."

"Yes, when he drank he became surly. And, often enough, he beat me for little reason."

"Did you begin to hate him?"

"Not enough to kill him."

"But maybe enough to have someone do it for you?"

"I think you had better leave Deputy Keller."

"Have I hit a nerve, Mrs. Holman? I hear you and Tilly Mathews are close friends. I also heard that her husband hung himself, I'm wondering if there is a connection."

"I want you out of here this minute."

"I could continue this down at the sheriff's office if you would like. Get your things, I'm taking you there if you won't answer my questions here." He said this as he was taking out his handcuffs."

Rachel could see she was in a tight place. She wouldn't want her friends to see her in handcuffs. They may take it that she killed her husband. She then changed her tone and said, "Maybe I was hasty, Deputy. Have a seat, I will answer your questions." "I don't think you killed your husband, Mrs.

Holman, but I think you may have knowledge of someone who did."

"I have no male friends, deputy."

"But you do have Tilly Mathews as a friend, and she is as strong as a man."

"She would be no match for Derrick. He was very strong. I ought to know, he beat me often enough." Her eyes were filled with hate."

"Yes, I see your hate for him in your eyes."

Kel left and went straight to Judge Coker. He told him about the interview and that he thought Rachel Holman would try to tip off Tilly Mathews. He asked for a court order to intercept the mail between these two. The order was signed, and given to the postmaster. He ordered his postal workers to give all local mail to him, as not to let his staff know whose mail he was looking through.

Just as Kel thought, a letter from Rachel Homan was sent to Tilly Mathews. The postmaster gave the letter to Judge Coker. He sent for Kel before he opened the letter. The letter read:

> Tilly,
>
> That new deputy was here asking questions about Derrick. He will probably be coming your way soon. Don't say a word. Just turn him away.
>
> Rachel

Kel said, "Judge, I think Tilly killed Derrick Holman.

I can't prove it, but I may be able to, after I talk to Tilly Mathews."

"If what you say is true, she may kill you, too, if you go out there alone. I recommend you take the sheriff with you."

"No, I think she would clam up, and we would get nothing. I'll be alright. I'll have the sheriff go with me until we are near her place, then wait for me in a stand of trees."

The Judge said, "I just hope you know what your doing, young man."

Kel talked it over with Sheriff Wilson, and he thought Kel had a good plan."

Kel arrived about noon the next day. Two dogs came to the picket fence that ran around the house. They were large vicious dogs that wanted to attack, but had been trained not to leave the picket fence.

As Kel rode up, Tilly came to the gate of the picket fence and said, "How can I help you, Deputy?"

Kel said, "I would like to talk to you about the disappearances of Derrick Holman and Deputy Andrews."

Tilly showed no signs of surprise and said, "Sure, Deputy, get down and come into the house. I'll chain the dogs up."

Kel got down and opened the gate and walked up to the door. Billy was inside and had a smile on his face.

Kel said, "Hello Billy," with a friendly smile and shook his hand."

When they were in the parlor, Tilly said, "Would you like a cool glass of lemonade and maybe a sweet roll?"

"Yes, please, but just the lemonade."

She was gone a minute or so, and was back with the lemonade. She was about to sit down, when Kel said, "I've changed my mind, I think I would like a sweet role. She left and Kel handed the glass of lemonade to Billy, He drank it down nearly in one gulp and handed it back to Kel. Kel sat the glass down on a coffee table, and smiled when Tilly returned.

He said, "I talked to Rachel Holman today, and she said some interesting things about her husband's disappearance and they involved you."

"That's right deputy. The other deputy said the same thing, and I made him disappear, also. You see that row of trees?" And they looked out the window. "There are men below two of them. I have Billy dig a hole eight feet deep, and three feet round. I dropped them into the hole and plant a tree over it. You will be in a hole soon, and will feed that tree for years."

"I don't think so, Tilly. You see I had Billy drink that lemonade. I hope it was knockout drops and not poison, for if it were poison, you just killed your own son."

She screamed and came at Kel, but he had risen, and just stepped aside. As he did he drew his gun and hit her on the head. He then walked over, dragged her into the kitchen and handcuffed her to a large pipe that came into the house. Billy was unconscious on the coach. Kel then got his horse and rode back to the sheriff and brought him.

As they rode, Kel explained what happened, and what Tilly had told him. When they arrived Tilly was sobbing. She knew she was done for, and Billy would be a ward of the court. Billy awoke and the sheriff told him to hookup the wagon as he needed to take his mother to town.

Tilly had resigned herself to her fate, and confessed everything, and how she did it. The bodies were exhumed and buried in the cemetery. Rachel was sentence to ten years in prison and Tilly was hanged.

Sheriff Wilson said, "You are a great detective, Kel. I've asked the commissioners to give you a ten dollar raise.

Thanks anyway, Sheriff, but I'm moving on to Austin. The college here is not for me. I think I want to be a lawyer.

CHAPTER 7
THE GROUP

The county commissioners gave Kel a thousand dollar bonus as Tilly's farm was sold and he was given the thousand dollars from Tilly's savings and the sale of the home. A family wanted Billy and he was awarded half the money.

Kel left San Antonio with a letter of recommendation from each county commissioner and one from Sheriff Wilson.

The trip to Austin was uneventful. Kel was amazed at the number of farms and small villages along the way. He thought, *"Texas is filling up with people. It's a great place to live."*

Austin was a growing city. It was around lunch when he came into town. While he was looking for a place to stay he saw Landon going into a pharmacy store. He followed him in and said, "Hello, Landon. Do you remember me?"

Landon stepped around the counter and embraced him. He said, "Your mother will be elated to see you, Kel. She says nearly everyday, how she misses you. I'll take you home right now."

Kel said, "She's living in Austin with you?"

"Yes, after she left Alton, she applied for a divorce. It took well over a year, but it was finally granted. We were married the next week. You see, Alton, had all but abandoned her. She was alone all but a couple of weeks a year."

"Yeah, I could see him changing. Getting more cattle was his only goal in life. He very seldom talked to me, and no one knew I was his son. I didn't want the other hands to know I was his son. I left him over a year ago and went to San Antonio."

"What did you do there?"

"I was hired as a night jailor, but later was promoted to a deputy. It's good work, but can be dangerous if you aren't particularly careful. I always was."

They traveled in a new buggy to a very large house. It sat on a large lot that was landscaped marvelously. A man was working in the yard when they arrived. The man got up from what he was doing, and took the reins from Landon when he stepped down.

Landon said, "Thank you, Alvin."

Alvin said, "Are you in for the day?"

"No, but it will be sometime before I leave. I'll hitch up the mare myself when I go."

When Landon opened the door, it was to a large room dressed with expensive furniture. Louise was coming into the room to see who Landon was talking with. When she saw Kel she ran to him. She cried and held him tightly.

She then backed away and said, "How did you find me?"

"I was coming to Austin to enter the college here, and saw Landon going into a pharmacy. I had no idea that you were in Austin or that you had married Landon."

"I have a lot to tell you, Son. Come into the library and we will talk. You may be disappointed in me after you hear it all."

She then told how she and Gracie were close friends. She said, "After Gracie died Landon and I became a couple. Alton never came home anymore and Landon was so kind to me that we fell in love. He sold his pharmacy and home in Marble Falls, and bought this house. I divorced Alton and later married Landon."

Landon said, "Let's tell it all, Louise. I want Kel to know all of it."

"You tell it Landon, I just can't."

Landon said, "Before you were born your mother and I fell in love. Gracie told your mother that she was glad we loved each other as she knew she was dying. She actually put us together. While Gracie was in Austin being treated, your mother and I were together. Kel, I'm actually your father."

Kel was visible shocked. He said, "I can see that now. I always wondered why I looked nothing like Dad. I don't think he ever noticed, because the only thing he thought of was how he could enlarge his ranches. Even John and Karl said that, too.

"It is a shock though, knowing you're my father. I can see why you left dad, mom. He has a Mexican woman that keeps his house in Fredericksburg, and he is much closer to her than he was to you.

"This world is strange. The little dad told about his father, it seems they were cut from the same cloth. I intend to break that tradition."

Landon said, "Kel said he came here to go to college, Louise." He then turned to her and said, "I want him to live with us. We have plenty of room, Kel, and it will not be an imposition for any of us. Your mother needs to be around you now, and I want us to know one another. What do you say?"

Kel grinned and said, "I was looking for a place to live when I saw you, Landon. I would love to be near mother again. We were always close."

"So it's settled. Louise show Kel his room, and I'll go get his things from the buggy."

Kel said, "I need to go when you go Landon, as my horse is at the livery stable."

Kel's room was upstairs at the end of a wide hallway. It was large and had a fireplace and a couch and soft chair facing it. It had a desk and chair, also. He had a private bath that contained a large tub. Louise opened a closet that was enormous.

Kel said, "I would have to be rich to fill that closet."

Landon then came into the room with Kel's things. Louise helped him put his few clothes away then said, "Let's have some coffee Are you hungry, Kel?"

"No Mom, but I would like some coffee."

As they went downstairs Kel noticed a beautiful grand piano in the great room. He said, "Wow, when did you get this?"

Louise said, "Landon bought it for me last Christmas. Actually he bought it for you, also, as he went to all your recitals with Gracie. He told me that you owned half of the piano as he loved your playing. Would you play something now for us, Kel?"

"Sure. I haven't played since I left Marble Falls. Gracie

always wanted me to go to Austin to study under a noted instructor."

"Well, you might just get that chance. There is a noted German director who leads the Austin's orchestra. I'm told he gives lessons to those who are gifted."

"Well, that leaves me out. He would laugh at my playing."
"I don't think so, Kel," Landon commented. "Gracie thought you had a gift and talked to me about it several times after you left from your lessons."

Louise said, "Sit down and try out your piano, Kel."

Kel sat and ran some scales before he played any musical piece. He found his fingers running over the keys like he had never quit playing. He then played a favorite of his mothers.

"You really have a touch, Kel," said Landon. He then said, "I've got to return to the pharmacy."

Kel left with him to get his horse. At dinner that night, he told how he wanted to enter college. All thought this was the right thing to do.

Unbeknown to Kel, Landon met with Igor Lichtenstein, also, known as The Professor. He told of his son wanting to take piano lessons from him. The professor said, "Let me set this up. I want my piano player in the orchestra to meet with him. I will be in the next room and listen to him go through some scales, then I will make my decision."

Landon told Kel that a man was interested in hearing him play, and had set up a time for Kel to be at his studio. Igor had come early, and was sitting by some French doors to the studio. He could see Kel's hands from his vantage point.

Kel came in and the man from the orchestra asked Kel to run through some scales. Kel's hands went through the scales at great speed. He was then given a page of sheet music that Kel had never seen. After studying the sheet for a moment, he then played it putting proper tempo and phrase of the music.

The professor then came into the room and introduced himself. He said, I am Professor Lichtenstein. I wanted to listen to you play before I committed to teaching you music. Your hands are skilled, and I will count it a privilege to teach you. We both have to commit to this or it is no good. I will require you to practice two hours each day. I will meet with you three times a week. I think we can be successful if we both commit to this routine."

"I have heard of you, professor, and it is an honor for you to take me on as a student. Do we have a goal to look for?"

"Yes, to make you into the best that you can be at the piano. I think you have potential. After six months, I will expect you to play in our orchestra along side Mr. Bernstein, here."

Kel turned and said, I will look forward to playing with you, Mr. Bernstein, and thanks for listening to me."

"I feel it will be me in a few years that will be thanking you for letting me play with you. You have a rare gift with those hands of yours. I shall look forward to our friendship."

At dinner that evening, Kel told the good news. He looked at Landon and said Mr. Bernstein told me that you set this up for me. Thank you."

"I felt that God gave you this gift, and it would be a sin not to follow it to the utmost." What Kel didn't know was that Landon compensated the professor quite well.

Kel entered college that fall. He was a pre-law student. Landon's house sat fairly close to the college, so Kel walked each day. In his first class he was seated by a girl of about eighteen. She turned to him and said, "I'm Cindy Newhart."

Kel said, "I'm Kelton Keller, Cindy, but please call me Kel."

Their professor then walked in and everyone became silent. After class Cindy said, "Are you a pre-law student like me?"

"Yes, I suppose you are the only woman studying law."

"No, there are two others. We all know each other, and have agreed to stick together."

"May I join you? I'm a cowboy, and need all the help I can get."

"Yes, the girls will love you to join our group. I won't ask you now, but we will all like you to tell us about your cowboy days. In return, we will help you with your studies if you need it. I know Greta and Lorie will be pleased. I'm meeting them at the student center. Would you join us?"

"Sure, I will look forward to meeting them."

At the center they walked to a table where two girls sat. Both were astonished that Kel was joining them. After being introduced, Cindy said, "Kel is a cowboy, and I know all of us want to hear you tell about being a cowboy."

"Well, you get up at daybreak and eat beans for breakfast. You saddle your horse and ride out to check on the cattle. You generally move the cattle from pasture to pasture to keep them on good grass. In the Spring you have to chase down all the ones that have strayed. Then you brand all the new calves and castrate the males. You also, check them for worms and sores."

Lorie asked, "What is castrate. I've never heard that term?"

"In polite talk, it means to remove their testicals, so they will be gentle and grow bigger."

"The girls were shocked and Kel could see they were. He then said, "We're all adults, and these are thinks that cowboys do. If one of you would have explained the term 'castrate,' no one would have been shocked. You would just have taken it as knowledge you didn't know.

"If I am to be part of your group, we need to set gender aside, and become one group. Our goal is to become lawyers. We must all help one another in reaching that goal. Me, being male, can help you as I can see things from a masculine view point, and you from a feminine. One rule would be that we never become involved with one another, as it would hurt the group. We never want to do that as it would impede our goal. Does this make sense?"

Lorie said, "That is what I would like. We don't have our parents anymore to guide us, so we must obtain guidance from the group. If we are having trouble or things look badly for one of us, we will come to the group to work it out. Having Kel with us will really help. I'm really beginning to see the wisdom of having a group."

Cindy said, "We know about ourselves as we grew up together, but we want to know more about you, Kel. Where did you go to school, Kel?"

"Marble Falls. My dad owns a ranch near there."

"Is your mother still there?" asked Greta.

"No she lives here in Austin and I live with her. Sometime soon, I will take you three to meet her. Do you all live in Austin?"

Lorie said "None of us lived in Austin until now. We all three are from Houston and grew up together. Cindy and my father are lawyers and are partners. So we may have a job when we graduate."

He turned to Greta and said, "What does your father do?"

She said, "He's a detective with the Houston police department."

"I was a deputy sheriff for over a year in San Antonio. I quit it so I could go to college."

"Did you wear a gun and have a badge."

"Of course. All deputy sheriff's wear a pistol and have a badge."

"Did you ever arrest someone."

"Yes, I arrested two women. They hanged one of them for killing three men and the other is serving ten years for conspiracy to commit murder."

"My, you don't look old enough to be a deputy sheriff."

"No, but I told the sheriff I was twenty-two as I needed a job. He probably knew I was under age, but he needed a deputy badly, and I had backed him up in an arrest that could have turned deadly. After that he had respect for me, as I probably saved his life."

"My, you have been around. Did you ever have to use your gun?"

"Yes, but I never used my gun unless there was no other way."

Greta said, "I like that. I'm going to tell my dad what you said. I'll bet he will like it. He tries to be as fair with people as he can be. I'm proud of him."

"I can see that."

They decided to meet three times a week and more if studying together helped. One of their meetings was held at

Landon's and Louise's house. The girls were amazed at the grandeur of the house. Kel introduced Landon and Louise as Mr. and Mrs. Howard, but Landon quickly said, "Please call us Landon and Louise or we will feel old."

The girls laughed and agreed to that.

Cindy said, "My what a beautiful piano, do you play, Louise?"

"Some, but the muscian in our family is Kel." All eyes went to him as Cindy said, "Please play for us, Kel."

Kel was embarrassed some, but he was a good sport and sat down and ran through three pieces that were international favorites. They all clapped. Kel then said, "We need to get at the business of why we are here."

Kel had explained to Landon and Louise about the group and their goal, so Louise had made a table in the library for a place they could meet. The group had one class that the professor made difficult.

They were now seated at the table and Greta said, it appears to me that a professor can make his class as easy or hard as he wants it to be."

Lorie said, "The objective of any professor should be to teach what he determines as the essentials his students must learn of his subject, not to make it difficult of easy."

"I think some of the professors get so wrapped up with their subject, that they don't see how it fits in the overall education of the student."

"I agree with you, Greta, but we need to tackle Professor Bowie's subject so he can see we reflect what he is trying to teach us." said Kel.

Cindy said, "I think the way to attack this is for each one

of us to have a conference with Professor Bowie. We should ask him directly what he wants to instill in each of us so we will be better lawyers."

"Excellent, Cindy. Let's now form the questions we should ask him to achieve that," said Kel.

They then spent the rest of their session forming the questions. Lorie said, "I think these questions may help professor Bowie as much as us."

The four made excellent grades as their confrences with their professors were tailored by the group to find out what he wanted from his students. Knowing this, they were able to reflect what was required on his tests.

CHAPTER 8
PROBLEMS

The girls lived in a dormitory. Lorie and Cindy lived together and Greta was next door. She missed a meeting now and then with the group, and when asked, she always had an excuse. What had happened was Greta had met a boy that she liked a lot. She was gone a lot from the dorm and Lorie and Cindy noticed.

They talked to Kel about it and he said, "She's seeing someone. I think we should confront her at the next meeting she attends, and have her lay her cards on the table."

"Let's do that, Kel, but in as loving a way as we can. If we accuse her, it will cause her to put her back up. We surely don't want that. I think you should lead this Kel as coming from you, it may be easier for her."

At the next group meeting that Greta attended Kel said, "Greta we have a problem."

Her demeanor quickly changed and she said, "What is the problem?" She said it in a defensive manner.

Kel said, "We want to solve this problem before it becomes a big problem as we all agreed to do this when we formed the group. Our goal is to become lawyers and anything that detracts from that, we think it should be discussed as a group. For if one of us needs help, the others will do anything in their powers to help the other one."

"I get it. You think I have a problem because I missed a few meetings."

"Not just that, but your grades are suffering. You have to ask yourself, 'Am I being honest with the group and our goal?'"

"Okay, I have a boyfriend. I'm not completely serious about him, but I'm getting to the point that I could be. I have questioned myself about it. Is it him or the group?"

"Life is complicated and you have asked the right question. Is he worth throwing your education away. What if it doesn't work out, then where will you be? My advise is to not see him for awhile, and see how you feel in a week or so. Also, it will see if he feels the same after not seeing you for awhile. Will you do that for the group. As I see it, this is a life changing decision."

Greta sat there awhile and no one said a word. After a bit, she said, "Out of respect for the group, I will tell him I need two weeks off from our relationship to evaluate it. Even if he protests, I will stick to it, out of respect for the group. I don't want anymore talking about this until the two weeks are over, then I will let you know."

Two weeks passed and Greta said, "It has been two weeks. My boyfriend took up with another girl. It hurt me badly, but it became clear to me he was not the one. However, I know I'm going to hurt for a long time."

Lorie put her arm around her and said, "If you were to

have left us we would have been hurt for a long, long time."
Greta cried then, and it brought tears to all their eyes.

Cindy said, "I think this brought our group closer together,
Greta. We found that we love each other more deeply."

Lorie always saw some humor in everything. She said,
"Kel, after we are lawyers you will have to marry us all."

Kel's music lessons went well, the professor had him play
fiery numbers, and then the sweet music of Franz Shubert.
He mastered them both. He gave a few proformances with
Professor Bernstein and they played duets that were greatly
received.

At the next group meeting Cindy said, "You were supposed
to tell the group if you ever fell in love and you haven't."

Kel was at a loss and said, "I don't even have a girlfriend."

"We know that Kel, but the way you played the piano
last Saturday night, we could all tell you are in love with the
piano."

Kel grinned and said, "I do love to play. I feel the music
expresses what I feel."

Lorie said, "I know, I feel about your music as you do. It
reaches deep inside of me and brings out love."

"That is exactly what I wanted to do, but never could put
it into words, Lorie."

Greta said, "Your music has brought the group closer
together. Once we are lawyers, I feel we should keep the group
together here in Austin, and form our own law firm. We may
be slow getting it started, but in the end, as a group, I think
we could conquer anything."

"I think you have a point," said Kel. What do you two
think?"

"She's right," said Greta, "We can do much better as a group than individually, as we trust each other. That's where the real strength is, we trust each another. We're like a good marriage and I feel I am married to the group."

Lorie said, "You just put into words what we all feel."

They graduated and all passed the bar the first time. They then opened their law firm. They borrowed a thousand dollars from Landon, and were able to qualify for a loan to buy a three storied building in the downtown district. The first floor was their offices and the two other floors were for their living space. Kel stayed living with Landon and his mother.

One of the ways they earned money when they were starting up, was Kel giving concerts where they charged. The girls advertised and ran the concert. Slowly their business began to grow. They hired a seasoned lawyer who was an alcoholic. They dried him out, and one of them was with him nearly all the time. His name was Patrick Abel. He was smart, and had years of experience. He was practically like a professor, as he helped them in numerous ways, especially in court. He had been a brilliant trial lawyer, until the bottle took control of his life. He was fired by a noted law firm, and no one would hire him.

Pat was Forty-five years old, and had a lot of gray in his hair. His children were grown and his wife had left him, and was now married and living in another city. Their business picked up considerably, as Pat became known once again for his skill.

They were appointed and paid by the state to defend people who could not afford an attorney. One was a woman,

Karen Isabel, who was arrested for killing her husband. When Lorie and Kel were interviewing her, she swore she had been framed.

Her husband was partners with a man. They owned a thriving department store.

They sold mostly clothes, but sold many other items. Karen said, her husband's partner, Wesley Herman, had asked to come over to discuss taking on another line of merchandise. She said she woke up just as the police were coming in their door. She had a pistol in her hand, and her husband was lying dead on the floor. The police took the gun from her and arrested her for murder.

"Wesley told the prosecutor that he was coming over to see his partner, when he heard a gunshot. He went directly to the police, as he was scared to go into the house. The police came in the front door, and there was Karen with the gun still in her hand. There was nothing she could do.

There was a woman's garter in her husband's hand that wasn't Karen's. She cooperated with the police. She said that Westley had come over, and she served them coffee. She then woke up to find her husband dead, and a gun in her hand.

Wesley said, "I never came into that house. When I heard the shot I went straight to the police."

There were no coffee cups or evidence that showed Wesley had been there. The front door was locked, and the police had to break in the door. There was nothing that showed that Wesley had been in the house.

The partners had a provision in their wills that said the other would inherit the other's half of the business should either one of them die. The prosecutor used the garter that was in Marvin's hand as a motive. He claimed that Karen had found out about an affair her husband was having, and killed him in a fit of rage.

Kel and Lorie interviewed both policemen who found Karen, and asked if she appeared angry. Both said no that she appeared as if she were just waking up. He then had the girls cover the pharmacies in Austin. There were only two, but when asked if any of the pharmaitist had sold knockout drops to anyone in the past month, neither had.

The group met and discussed the crime. Kel said, "The prosecutor will use the garter as motive, but we must interview at least five of Karen's friends to see if she had a temper. If we can put five of them on the stand that shows she didn't have a temper, that will help our case.

"I was able to get a copy of Marvin's will, and Wesley's will probably reads the same. It says if either of them die, the other inherits the business free and clear. Wesley now has a motive and Karen doesn't. We now need to prove Wesley was in Karen's house. Wesley is now single as his wife passed away over a year ago."

Cindy said, "Maybe he killed her, too. That may be easier to prove than Marvin's murder."

Lorie said, "That may be true, but we would be starting from scratch there, and that was over a year ago, and the trail of evidence will be harder to recover."

Kel said, "I think we should cover all the pharmacies within a fifty mile radius of Austin. There can't be that many. I will ask Landon. He will know them all."

They obtained the list, and there were only four. One pharmacy was in Marble Falls, another in Georgetown, another in Round Rock and the last in Bastrop. Kel said he would cover Marble Falls and Georgetown. Greta went to Round Rock and Lorie to Bastrop.

They were able to get a picture of Wesley from the newspaper, as he had run for the city council a couple of years back, and they had his picture. They had three photos made that were eight by ten and were a good likeness of Wesley.

Kel found nothing in Marble Falls and Georgetown. It was the same for Lorie in Bastrop. However, Greta asked the pharmacy in Round Rock, and they had sold two bottles of the drops. Both were for capturing wolves. Greta showed the photo of Wesley and the man said, "Yes, that's one of the men who bought knockout drops." All were elated with the find.

They then traced the gun. They went to every gunsmith like they had the knockout drops, but turned up nothing there. They then asked the clerks that were employed at the department store. They told them that they were not to mention the interview to anyone, even their wives. They asked each if they had ever seen Wesley with a pistol. None had, but then a janitor said, "I hate to admit this, but I was looking for a drink one night, and thought Mr. Herman may have a bottle in his desk. When I was going through his desk, I saw a thirty-two, snubbed nosed Colt."

At the trial they brought in five women who testified that Karen was mild mannered, and had never shown any anger as long as they had known her. The prosecutor then asked if Karen had ever mentioned being jeolous. He then broght in a witness who said he had seen Marvin on occasion, having a drink at the bar across the street from the department store, but on cross examination the man said he was never with a woman or talked to one.

They then brought in the pharmacist who sold the knockout drops to Wesley. As they had to submit their witness list before the trial, the prosecutor got with Wesley and he said he used the drops on cats that were envading his house.

Kel on cross examination said, "You told the pharmacist that you were buying the knockout drops to trap wolves. Why didn't you tell him you were using them to trap cats.

Herman said, "I was afraid he might not sell me the drops if he loved cats."

Kel said, "This proves our point that Mr. Herman was in possession of knockout drugs and could have used them on Mrs. Isabel and her husband."

The prosecutor said, "I object to Mr. Keller's statement. Knockout drugs are not part of this trial."

The Judge said, "Where are you going with this Mr. Keller?"

Kel said, "I will have the police officers who were first on the scene, and they will testify that Mrs. Isabel appeared to be just waking up. So if that is true she may have been drugged with knockout drops."

The prosecutor said, "Those officers are not experts on that subject."

Kel said, "Anyone can tell if someone is just waking up, because they are groggy.

Kel said, "We contend that Mr. Herman put drops in both Marvin and Karen Isabel's drinks and staged the whole crime scene."

The prosecutor yelled his objected, and it was sustained and ordered the jury to disregard Kel's statement.

Kel then asked, "Why would you go clear to Round Rock to buy the knockout drops when there are pharmacies here in Austin?"

Wesley hemmed and hawed a bit, then said he went up to Round Rock to see a friend."

Kel said, "What is your friend's name?"

"Malcom Davis."

"Is Malcom Davis still in Round Rock?"

"No, he moved back East, and I don't have his address now."

"Very convenient. But we are still going to cover Round Rock to see if anyone there knew Malcom Davis."

They then brought in the janitor who had seen the pistol in Wesley's desk. Kel asked the janitor what kind of a pistol was it?"

The janitor replied, "A snub nosed Colt, thirty-two."

Kel said, "Did I at anytime ever mentioned anything about the pistol, other that it was a pistol?"

"No, but I know guns and could tell immediately it was a thirty-two."

The prosecutor said, "I think the defendant's council put the name of the pistol in your head."

The janitor rose up from the stand and said, "Are you calling me a liar?"

The judge then said, "Strike the prosecutor's statement from the record as it is out of line. If you do that again counselor, I will find you in contempt. Do you understand me?"

The prosecutor nodded, and the judge almost shouted, "Do you understand me?"

The prosecutor said, "Yes."

In there summations Kel said, "There is much more evidence that points to Wesley Herman as being the murderer than Karen Isabel. The policemen who found her, said she looked like a person who had just awakened. The will of the two partners show's Mr. Herman's motive. The motive presented by the prosecutor was only a garter that was likely planted as was the gun in Mrs. Isabel's hand. The janitor identified the exact caliber of gun that was used to commit the murder. Then there's the fact that Mr. Herman bought knockout drops in Round Rock when he could have bought them here in Austin.

There is no motive for Mrs. Isabel to kill her husbund of twenty-five years. You heard the ladies testify to her demenor as mild. The proscecution only point is that Mrs. Isabel had the gun in her hand. The police officer testified it was cold showing it hadn't been fired for some time.

What person would still have a murder weapon in their hands an hour after a murder?" There is much more evidence that Mr. Herman committed the murder, than Karen Isabel. You must aquite her on the grounds I have shown you."

The prosecutor said, "The defense is just trying to confuse you with a lot of things that have nothing to do with the fact that Mrs. Isabel had the murder weapon in her hand and her husband was dead on the floor. The garter in Mr. Isabel's hand shows motive. He was evidently having an affair and was confronted by his wife, and she shot him dead.

Those facts are before you, so any reasonable person can see she is guilty as charged."

The jury was out less than a half hour and Karon Isable was found innocent of all charges.

The case had been publicized in the Austin American and was headlines. The law office of Evans, Hinds, Keller and Newhart was now on the map.

CHAPTER 9

RUMORS OF WAR

The group still met once a week by themselves. At a meeting Cindy brought up the rumors of war that were circulating. Cindy said, "The way the talk is going, war could breakout at anytime. Pat said he was talking to a man from Atlanta who said a militia is forming here in Texas. Texas will go with the South I'm sure. They will want Kel to go with them. He's twenty-seven, and a natural leader, so they will want and demand he come with them."

Kel said, "No one but you people know I do not hold with slavery, and could never fight to preserve that. I have purposely kept my feeling to myself as most people think otherwise."

Lorie said, "I think you should leave Austin sometime soon. That way they will not think you left to avoid the army."

Greta said, "Where would you go if you left?"

"I surely don't want to be a cowboy again. That life is very hard and I have become soft living in Austin, and I don't want to go back into law inforcement."

Lorie said, "Why don't you tell everyone that you are going back East to pursue a musical career."

Cindy said, "That really sounds good, Lorie, and it's

something that everyone will believe, Kel. The only things we need to decide now is when and where are you going."

"My, you girls aready have my bags packed. I do see the need to leave. I hate to leave the group, but sometimes bad things happen. I think I can wrap up the cases I'm on, and turn the others over to you. Don't tell anyone the real reason I'm leaving. Just let that be our secret."

Greta said, "I have another item we need to discsus. Alvin is back in Austin and I've been seeing him. He wants me to marry him.

"He said he has gone with numerous women since we broke up, and he always thinks of me. He told me that the greatest thing he missed was our conversations. He said I was more than someone he was attracted to, he said being my friend was the biggest part."

"Do you love him, Greta?"

"Yes, No one else will do."

"Then grab him before he gets away," said Lorie, and everyone laughed.

Greta said, "I want to marry him before you leave, Kel. I want the whole group behind me when I marry."

Kel sid, "Thanks, Gerta. You had better tell him about our group, and what it means to you. I compare our group to the Lord. Nothing supercedes our love for the Lord. The group comes next to me. It means that much to me."

Lorie said, "I feel the same way. Nothing in life gives me the security that I feel with three people behind me."

Cindy said, "I feel the same. Both Lorie and I date men, but I don't think I could ever feel the security I feel with the group behind me."

Kel said, "Now, I won't have that. You're turning me out into the world, and it will be lonesome and without security."

Greta said, "The war won't last a year, I'm told. The North has an army that will crush the South."

Cindy said, "I don't know. That's what England thought about we rebels in America. That war lasted a long time because America wanted independence. I see the South as the same. Patrotism will run an army for a long time."

"I hope in two years, everything will be back to normal, and I can return to Austin. I know mother won't like me leaving."

"No, she still thinks of you as her little boy, and will until you're sixty or better," said Cindy, and everyone laughed. Then she said, "I feel the same way, I don't like it a bit you being gone. All three of us will worry as much as your mother."

Lorie said, "Before you leave, please talk with Pat about going to Washington D.C. He is very wise, and may give you an idea of what you should do."

Kel met with Pat and explained why he was leaving, and that he thought he might go to Washington D.C. to find a job.

Pat was not quick to answer, but then said, "If you could counsel with Vice President Johnson, it might help. He's a Southerner, and will understand your situation and have some good advice."

***

Greta's marriage went well. There were many people there. All the parents of the girls came from Houston along with many of Greta's kin. She had two maids of honor.

Kel left a day later. He was heading for Washinton D.C. Pat had told him to look around for awhile before he applied to one of the government agencies. Pat had told Kel that with his law degree he could probably catch on with the attorney generals office, but to look around first to see what fit him best.

As Kel was throwing things into his suitcase, he saw his pistol and scabbard. He thought, *"You never know,"* and put them in his suitcase.

He had thought he would take the stage to Houston, and then catch a ship to New York City. It seemed like a good way to go. The first night the stage stopped at a stage station that provided a place to sleep. The station was in a small ranch town without a hotel. As they stopped about dinner time, he had dinner at the stage station. One of the passengers was an elderly man, who made conversation with Kel. He introduced himself as Wiley. They were standing outside the station and Wiley said, "I would like a drink before I turn in. There's a saloon not far away, will you accompany me?"

Kel said, "Why not."

As it was chilly Kel said, "I'll just be minute, I want to get a jacket." Kel was wearing a fedora hat, that he often wore in Austin. He hadn't taken his western hat as he thought it would be out of place in the East.

When he opened his suitcase and picked up his suit coat, he spotted his pistol. He thought, *"Better safe than sorry,"* and strapped it on under his suit coat. He checked his pistol, and it was clean and loaded. The coat hid his scabbard, but he tied down the bottom of the scabbard to his leg out of habit.

They reached the saloon and it had about seven or eight

men at the bar. They chose a place away from the men, and both ordered a rye. As they were about to toast one another. A man from the group of men down the bar said, "What have we here? A dude from the city."

Kel ignored him and clinked glasses with Wiley.

The man said, "I'm talking to you, Dude. So look at me."

Kel pushed his coat around back of his pistol, and while holding his glass in his left hand, pushed the leather thong off the hammer. He then said, "I want no trouble, Sir, I just want to have a quiet drink with my partner."

"The hell you say. You're too good to talk to me?"

"No Sir, I just want to be left alone," and looked back at Wiley who had a frightened look on his face."

The man then shouted, "Do you know who I am?"

"Yes, just a target if you want to push this. However, let me warn you, I'm good with a gun."

Two of his friends stepped up and one of them said, "How good are you with three?"

"Just as good. Please think before you make this into something big. I'll apologize if that will satisfy you. I despise violence, and will ask you to please let it go."

The first man said, "Maybe we don't want to let it go," and moved his hand near his gun.

Kel said, "If you touch that gun, I will kill you, and if I have to, both your friends."

The three all laughed, but Kel never took his eyes off the men's hands. Just then, the first man went for his gun, and an instant later both of his friends did, also.

It was just a blur as Kel shot the first man, and with his off hand fanned the hammer of his pistol killing both the other men. Not two seconds had elapsed. One of the men got a shot off, but it went into the floor. Smoke filled the area. Kel was feeding three more bullets into his pistol, then put it in his scabbard. In just a minute the sheriff rushed into the bar. He had expected trouble from the men from the GW ranch, but had surely not expected a killing.

Sheriff Tom Bradley said, "What happened Loris?"

Loris, the bartender, repeated verbatim what was said. He added, "Caleb drew first as did his friends, but they were no match for the dude."

"Who are you?"

"I'm lawyer from Austin. I haven't had a gun in my hands for over eight years, but I still know how to use it."

"That's obvious. Are you passing through?"

"Yes, I'm on the stage, and just came down to have a drink with one of my fellow passengers. I repeatedly told the men I wanted no trouble, but they pushed it. I'm very sorry it came to this, but I had no choice."

The sheriff said, "Loris have Dick come and get these men. You, Mister Lawyer, come down to the office, I have some papers for you to sign. Loris, you can come down when you can as a witness."

Wiley never said another word. He left as the sheriff and Kel went to the sheriff's office.

When Kel returned to the stage station, Wiley was outside with a bottle. Kel said, "Please don't mention this to anyone. I hate violence, but somehow it's sometimes put on me and I have no choice."

Wiley still said nothing. Kel could tell he was shaken. He did hand the bottle to Kel and he took a drink and handed it back. They stood outside for another half hour in silence, then turned in.

Kel reached Houston and was able to obtain passage on a ship two days later. He was glad to be aboard ship and alone again. The salt air was just what he wanted.

He reached New York and immediately caught a train to Washington D.C.

He was touring the capital building when a young lady who was the daughter of a government official saw him. She had been to one of his concerts in Austin, and was rapt with his talent.

She boldly walked up to him and said, "Mr. Keller, I'm Amy Mercer. My father is with the commerce department," actually he is the secretary of commerce. We were in Austin a year ago, and I came to a concert you were giving. I must hear you again. If I arrange for you to play for a group of us, would you at least consider it?"

"I'm flattered Miss Mercer. I will consider it, because of you."

"Will you give me your address? I am so glad you are here in Washington. Are you just visiting or are you going to live here?"

"I don't really know. I'm a lawyer by trade, and decided I would like to work for the U. S. government, so I'm looking around."

"Oh, I hope you decide to stay. Washington will be so much richer with your talent. I can't wait to tell my father. He was as fascinated with your music as mother and I were. Would you give me your address?" Kel gave her the name of his hotel.

The next day he received an invitation to have dinner at the Mercer residence. He was there promply at six as the invitation stated. He was dressed in a light blue blazer with dark blue pants and a white shirt and tie. He looked very good.

He was amazed at the number of people there. He found that dinner was at seven, but Mr. Mercer wanted to introduced him to his friends. There were several of the presidents cabinet there.

The Mercers had a grand piano, and of course he was asked to play. He knew he would probably be asked, and thought of the music he would play. He wowed them. Everyone was awed with his talent. Mercer said, "Didn't I tell everyone that Mr. Keller had the talent of a master?"

Dinner went well. Amy was with her fiancé, named Wendell Carey. As he shook Kel's hand he said, "You won't take my Amy away from me will you?"

Kel laughed and said, "I think she wants more than a piano player as a husband," and they both laughed."

The word spread about Kel's talent. He was amazed that he was invited to the White House to play for President Linclon. He of course sent word that he would be delighted. On a Satruday night he performed before thirty or so people, all of which were in Lincoln's inner circle. He was introduced to Vice President Johnson.

Kel said, "Mr. Vice President, may I meet with you about a private matter?" Johnson said, "Of course. Please come to my office on Monday morning. I will see that my calendar is moved around so I can see you around ten, if that will please you."

"Thank you for your kindness. I will be there."

On Monday Kel explained to Johnson that he was from Texas, but did not hold with slavery. He said, "I cannot fight for a cause I do not believe in, but neither do I want to fight against my own. So you see the predicament I find myself in."

"I see your situation and it is much like my own. I've been told you're a lawyer by trade, so getting a job in Washington will be easy. I will introduce you to Ed Stanton. He's the attorney general. I think if you will talk with him, and tell him what you told me, he will find a place for you that is not war related. After all there are still a lot of people breaking the law, and he needs smart people to help him put them away. So you see you would be doing your country a favor, and still not betray your people."

Three week later, Kel received a note from Ed Stanton to meet with him in his office. Kel went there and they talked for sometime.

Stanton said, "I did a little research on you before we talked. I found you were a cowboy and a deputy sheriff in San Antonio, where you solved a crime that no one else could solve. You then moved on to Austin, and became a lawyer in your own law firm. You have an impeccable record Mr. Keller. Any agency in Washington would want your services. I am lucky enough to have first crack at you.

"I would like to employ you as a special investigtator. That may work into something greater, but at this time I am particularly in need of a smart, young person, who can obtain some information that I would dearly love to have. It seems someone or a group is selling arms to the Southern states. I would like to know who and where. I don't want you to confront anyone, I just want their names and where the arms are coming from. I've had some agents on this for sometime, but neither of the agents came up with anything. Would you like to give it a try? I can promise that you will be compensated handsomely."

"Thank you for the offer. It sounds like something I would like to try. When would you want me to start?"

"Monday. I want you to use an alias as this could come back to bite you, if you pursue a career here in Washington. I see you as a man of action. You could help your country a great deal, while not compromising your love of the state of Texas. You Texans have a fierce love for your state. More so than any other state. It must be the close bond with your neighbors.

"There is some training that is necessary. We want you to be able to identify every weapon available. We have an expert on weapons who will spend a week with you. At the end of a week, we feel you will have a grasp of every weapon available.

CHAPTER 10

BOSTON

Kel arrived in Boston using the name of John Kelly. He found a suitable place to live in a boarding house. A Mrs. Ashton owned and ran the boarding house. She was a widow in her mid forties. She had five other boarders. Kel decided to be friendly, but not mix with them socially.

The only woman who lived at the boarding house was a Miss Lidia Walton. She worked at a pharmacy that was owned by her uncle. She was trim and proper. She attended a church on Sunday and sang in their choir. She was cool, and had very little to do with the men. She did talk to Mrs. Ashton.

There was Linton Brodwell who worked for the Baltimore and Ohio Railroad. He was a widowed trainmaster. He was gone a great deal of the time, as his job took him out of town quite frequently.

Colin Tredwell was a clerk in a hardware store and Robert Hayward was also a clerk, but in department store. Neither were married.

The last was Calvin Quinn who worked as a supervisior of dock workers. He was quite friendly, but talked mostly to

Colin and Robert, as Kel had little to say and though not cold, was not engaging either.

As Mrs. Ashton introduced Kel at his first meal with the group, he was asked what he did. He replied, "I buy and sell weapons."

"What kind of weapons?" Quinn asked.

"All weapons, big and small. I like to buy in quantity as I have many clients both here and abroad."

Colin Tredwell said, "Well, your business may pick up, as I hear rumors of war all the time by individuals at the dock."

"Oh, what kind of rumors?" Kel queried.

"Why war with the South, of course. I hear they want to separate from the Union."

"Why would there be a war? They can just not participate with the other states and leave it at that."

Hayward said, "You should run for office. That is the best solution, I've heard."

Miss Walton said, "I see you have a Southern accent, Mr. Kelly, are you from the South?"

"I was raised in Texas until I was eighteen, then left for the Northeast to make money. Things were too slow in Texas, and as you can see, I'm no cowboy," which made all laugh.

"Lately, I find that buying and selling weapons is quite lucrative. I used to sell hardware, but you'll never get rich doing that."

Tredwell said, "I can attest to that." Then laughingly said, "Maybe you will need a partner?"

"You say that in jest, but I may need someone if the demand picks up because of the unrest."

The discussion then went to the probability of war. Kel

kept out of it, excused himself and left for his room. He had aquired a shoulder holster for a thirty-two snubnosed Colt. It fit under his coat, which kept it hidden quite well. He had a badge and identification that he was U. S. Marshal at large for the attorney general. He kept those in a hidden pocket in case he was searched.

He left the boarding house that was located near the dock. He saw an advertisement of a show being played at an upscale playhouse. He was able to purchase a ticket that was quite pricy. He entered a large room that had numerous tables. There he was placed at a table with several other people. The table was near the stage, and Kel's seat faced the stage. The opening act was a beautiful woman singer who was quite personable as she came off the stage as she was singing. She came by Kel's table as she sang. It was conspictous that he was alone, so the singer began looking into his eyes as she sang a love song.

Kel wasn't embarrassed, as some men may have been, and looked back at her and smiled as she sang. When the song was over, Kel reached for her hand and said, "Why don't you join our party for a drink?"

She smiled and said, "Maybe some othertime."

"Kel said, "You may be passing up a chance of a life time, as these are important people."

She looked at them, and they were all dressed eloquently. She said, "Maybe one drink after I change."

When she left Kel said, "Thank you for not exposing me."

The obvious leader of this group said, "I like your style. Now we have Joan Rydell joining our party. What a treat. I can't wait to tell Martha about this. I'm Stanton Graves, and these are my partners, Jim and Les Tyson. These women work with us, and we are treating them to this show as a celebration of our tenth year in business. They have made me a lot of money over the years, and should be treated royally. These young girls certainly wouldn't be out with old codgers like us, unless it was a company party. They are respectable and I know their families."

"What busisness are you in Mr. Graves?

"We sell gunpowder and explosives."

"With the unrest with the South, you may increase your business dramatically."

"What do you do, Mr........"

"Kelly. John Kelly. I deal in weapons, Mr. Graves, so I see we are practically in the same business."

"Maybe not in the same business, but we may have the same clients."

"I view this as an opportunity for us both, Mr. Graves."

"Oh, how is that?"

"We could scratch each others backs when we are dealing with clients, and promote one another."

"You do have a head for business, Mr. Kelly. Please drop by my office when you have a chance," and he handed Kel a business card. "I would like to continue this conversation, but now I see Joan Rydell, you are a lucky man, Mr. Kelly."

Kel rose as did the other men as Miss Rydell approached. Kel took her hand and said, "Miss Rydell, this his Mr. Stanton Graves. He is treating his staff to a party for making him wealthy."

Stanton said, "And your escort is Mr. John Kelly a distinguished friend."

"How nice of you to ask me to your celebration," replied Joan.

Kel then seated her as a waiter came over. Kel had noticed a woman drinking a fruit cocktail that he had seen before and said, "Would you like to have a fruit coctail from the islands, Miss Rydell?"

"That would do nicely, Mr. Kelly."

Kel said, "Would you others like a fruit cocktail, also. The girls nodded and Kel said, "Bring us eight of them, please."

Joan said, "I see by your accent you are from the South, Mr. Kelly."

"Not the South, Miss Rydell, Texas. I was reared in Texas, and was never able to lose the accent."

"Oh, don't try to lose it, I adore it. I travel a lot, and find other accents delightful. It is kind of a hobby of mine."

"So how did you become a singer, Miss Rydell?"

"I was raised just north of here in Georgetown, and was selected to go to a conservatory. I was not suited for the opera, so I began singing here and there. I engaged an agent and moved along quite nicely."

Graves said, "All of us have heard about you, Miss Rydell, and count it an honor to have you at our table."

The drinks arrived, and they were delightful. Kel leaned over to the waiter and said, "Keep them coming when you see someone about to finish their drink."

The waiter winked at him and said, "You've got it, Captain."

Joan was near enough to hear the waiter refer to him as "Captain" and said, "Here I am out with a captain."

Before he could correct her. One of the girls said, "Let's

drink to Captain Kelly." Which they did and Kel just let it pass.

From then on they referred to him as "Captain." The drinks kept coming, and the waiter kept one in front of everyone who finished a drink. Kel noticed this, however, and slowed down on his drinking. Joan didn't notice, as did the others, and after the second drink, they were all considerably loaded.

Joan said, "Would you see me backstage, Captain, I seem to be drunk, and need your assistance."

They left and Joan took him to her dressing room. There was no one there as the show had ended over a half hour ago. As they entered the door, Kel said, "I had best see you home, Miss Rydell. I think you may need me."

"Yes, I do need you," and came into his arms, and kissed him passionately. She retrieved her coat, and they walked across the street to her hotel. She was on the first floor and handed Kel her key. He unlocked the door, and she pulled him in and closes the door. She then pulled him over to a sofa and they sat. She kissed him again, then said, "Are you married?"

"No, and haven't been kissed in a long time. That was a very nice jesture to kiss me. I had better be going, as I think I took unfair advantage of you with the fruit drinks."

"A gentleman. My, I really hit the jackpot tonight. I will be speaking the lines that you ought to be saying, but I've thrown caution to the wind, tonight. Will you see me tomorrow?"

"For lunch if you'd like. I'll call for you at your room at twelve."

She said, "It's a date, Captain. You have done something to me."

"Yes, I got you drunk and I'm not proud of it. I want you to know me. I have never had a girlfriend."

"Never. My you have led a sheltered life. I want to know all about you."

Kel left and was thinking. *"She's been around, being in show business. I wonder what she's really like? I could have stayed, but that would be taking advantage of a woman who needed a friend more than a lover."*

The next day at lunch, Kel said, "Do you see us as a couple, Joan?"

"Maybe, but first I want you to know some things about me. You may want to back off. I'm twenty-six years old, and have been in show business for six of those years. I have had four lovers in my past. Two were married, but unknown to me. Another became so sick he had to be cared for by his parents. The fourth after a few months just backed away. So you see you're girlfriend has been around. I wouldn't blame you if you backed off because of my past."

"What you have done is small compared to what I have done. I was taught to use a pistol by my partner in my cowboy days. About a year after I was on the ranch, we were confronted by four men from another ranch. A dispute ensued over the ownership of some cattle. I could have backed away, and let them have the cattle, but I didn't. One of the men drew on me and I killed him.

"My partner said, 'Even though you were in the right, as he drew on you, it was actually murder, because of your skill with a pistol.' I decided then and there to quit my job as that kind of thing would come up again. I moved to Austin, Texas and went to college to become a lawyer. I then decided to leave Austin as I knew a war was coming and I didn't hold with slavery. I couldn't fight for something I didn't think was right. So, I came here to avoid that.

"However, as I was coming here, about two months ago, I killed three men. True they accosted me, and provoked the fight, but I know how deadly I am with a pistol. Afterward I remember what my partner said, 'that it was murder.' I have to live with the fact that I took four men's lives from this earth. So you see you are dining with a murderer. You're having been a bit promiscuous, seems like small potatoes compared to what I've done."

Joan was silent for awhile. She was truly shocked, and Kel could tell that she was. He let her digest what he had said, and decided not to speak until she did."

When she did speak she said, "What you did was forced upon you. What I did was calculated sin. I wanted you last night, and did all I could to get you to make love to me. I just read Nathanial Hawthorne's new book called *The Scarlet Letter*. It's a story of a woman, Hester Prynne, who had the letter "A" carved onto her breast that stood for adultery. I sometime think I should have that letter carved onto my breast."

"You do have a scar, not on you breast, but in your mind. I want to help you erase that letter. I know you would not concider going to a clergyman for help, but in my limited knowledge of what I know about the Bible, that is exactly why Christ came and died on the cross. It was to pay for your sins. My mother told me that when you confess your sins to

Christ, that he will forgive those sins. If God forgives your sins you should not keep carrying them."

"I have confessed my sins to Jesus, but then last night, had you stayed, I would have sinned again."

"My mother also told me that when you accept Christ into your heart, and confess your sins. He forgave not only the sins you have committed, but all the sins you are going to commit. We are all weak. I could not stand the humiliation, so I killed instead. I have later thought it would have been better if they killed me. At least I would never kill again."

"Maybe killing those men, was an act of God. They may have killed many other people had you not ended their lives. You will never know if God intended for you to kill them, but I believe he used you to complete his will.

"This is the deepest conversation I have ever had. I think this in itself is the will of God. I believe he sent you here to minister to me and I to you. I want to be near you the rest of my life. We may not marry or even become sweethearts, but we have this bond between us now. I'll try to keep you from killing men and you will help me to stop sleeping with every good looking man I see." This made Kel smile.

He said, "What God has joined together, let no man put asunder." As they were sitting side by side, Joan leaned over and hugged him while kissing him on the cheek. Kel said, "Being we are telling each other our deepest secrets, I want to tell you about a group I have been in for several years. It started the first day I attended college. I met a girl named Cindy Newhart. She then introduced me to two other girls who were from her hometown of Houston, Texas.

"We were all majoring in prelaw, wanting to become

lawyers. We took every class together throughout college. We formed a group. We would have conferences with every proffessor who taught us. By doing this, we could extract exactly what the professor wanted from us on exams. We all made A's in most of the subjects. We studied together, which brought us to discuss anything that was bothering us. I mean everything. They are the closest people in life to me.

"They decided that I should come East to avoid being in the Texas army which will join the South if they leave the Union. I do not hold with slavery, so they told me to go East."

"Were you ever envolved with any of them."

"No, they were like sisters. No, not even that. Closer than that, but platonic. I don't think I ever had a lustful thought about any of them. All were beautiful, to me."

"Will you go back to them at sometime?"

"Yes, I feel lonesome without them. Have you ever wanted your mother when you were far away?"

"Yes, I still want her at times, so I know how you feel. I would like to be like your group to you, John. I want to feel you close to me and be near you."

"Are you in love with me, Joan?"

"I hadn't thought of that, but yes, I think I am and I love the thought."

CHAPTER 11

THE ARMS COMPANIES

The next Monday, at ten o'clock, Kel was in Grave's office. He said hello to those who were at the celebration, and they all smiled at him. He was then shown into Grave's office.

Kel said, "I don't have any contacts yet, but I was hoping you could put me in touch with the arms dealers and ammunition companies you deal with. While calling on them, I will put in a good word for you."

"I like that Mr. Kelly. It's like having an employee I don't have to pay. I hope we can do a good deal of business together."

"I do, too. Contacts are the art of this business. The more contacts, the more business, and the more business the more profit."

"I would like to keep close contact with you. I saw you in action at the club. You got a celebrity to have drinks with you, and then showed her to her dressing room. We were all amazed. That is the most beautifully and talented woman I have ever seen or heard. I bet she makes more than I do. Will you see her again?"

"I hope to, but you never know. Show people put on a good face, on and off the stage."

Kel left with a list of manufacturers, dealers and ammunition makers, most of which were in or near to Boston. He also went to the docks and told the foreman of a longshoreman's gang that he would like to buy him a drink after work.

The foreman's name was Jack Albright. Jack took him to a saloon where many of the longshoremen did their drinking. After they had a pint of ale in front of them, Kel said, "I'm an arms dealer by trade. Are there many weapons being shipped lately."

"Not that you could see, but I know what arms being shipped look like, and there are plenty being shipped as hardware."

"As arm's dealers are competitors of mine, I like to keep tabs on them. If you want to make some money, and not break the law while you're doing it, jot down who is sending the arms and to whom. You will be paid ten dollars the next time I see you for that information. One other thing, keep what you are giving me under your hat. These people can be vicious sometimes."

"This brought a shocked look to the foreman's face. He said, "Thanks for the tip Matey, I see what you mean. Easiest money I ever made. Check with me each week and I'll have them for you. Thanks for the ale."

Kel didn't stop with that foreman. He met several other foreman and gave them the same deal. Each time, he warned them not to share what they were doing or they may meet with disaster. By the end of the week he had the information he wanted. He composed the names of the companies who were sending arms and who were receiving the shipments. He put the information in a large envelope and sent it to Attorney General Stanton.

Every night he met Joan, and he could tell she was in love with him. He loved her, but knew she loved him much more. As they were talking one night, Joan said, "I want you to stay with me. Having you for a few hours is not like having you most of the time."

"Are you suggesting marriage?"

"Yes, If you won't live with me any other way. I need you."
"Do you want a big wedding with your mother and father there?"

"No. My career can't have the interuption that would take. Can we just have a civil wedding, and not make it a big thing. I know my manager would not be in favor of it at this time. How do you feel about a civil wedding?"

"With your career, I can see the interruption at this time would not be good. I may be a little old fasion, but I need to be married to you if I am to sleep with you."

"She smiled and said, "I'm off tomorrow, lets do it then."

So they were married, and became a couple. Kel loved Joan, and could see she was deeply in love with him. He thought, *"If she needs me that badly, I will try and make her happy."* They found an apartment that was near her work and the docks.

As Kel investigated the names of the arms dealers who were sending arms to the South, he saw that Graves was involved with them. It appeared that they were organized. Although Kel had never confided with Graves on the subject, he noticed he asked probing questions. This alerted Kel to the fact that Graves was probably envolved.

Although he had been warned to never get involved with these dealer, he did a little probing himself, and traced the arms back to a central company who was doing the shipping. There were four arms dealers and Graves' gunpowder that were being shipped to Richmand, Virginia. He found the quantity, and was now working on the different arms that were being shipped.

Unknown to Kel, one of the foreman he had contacted, had a cousin who worked for one of arms dealers that were making shipments, and had tipped his cousin off. The cousin in turn, had talked to his boss about it. This activated an investigation of Kel.

Kel's birthday was coming up, and Joan wanted to surprise him by taking him out to dinner. She waited in a small alcove by their front door and had planned to grab him as he was about to enter their apartment which opened onto the street.

He heard her dress rustle, and turned, and she in one leap came into his arms to embrace him. Just as she did, a shot rang out and hit her squarely in her back. The bullet went through her, and hit the scabbard of his shoulder holtster as he had turned just as she came to him.

Joan was dead on the impact of the rifle bullet. As the door was partially open, Kel dragged Joan into the opening, but there was not another shot.

A policeman was just down the street, and ran to the apartment where the door was still open. He saw Kel holding Joan, rocking back and forth, as if he were cuddling a baby. The policeman had his gun out, and was now looking back out the door for the person who fired the shot. He blew his whistle loudly, and other policemen were now showing up.

A doctor was called, and he called for a mortician. They asked Kel to come down to the station and Kel went over what had happened. Kel didn't divulge anything about his involvement with the attorney general. The police then believed it was just a chance discharge of a rifle, and no charges were filed.

Kel had married Joan under the name of John Kelly, so if the police were to investigate him, all they would come up with, would be that he was married to Joan.

Joan's parents arrived, but Kel just told them he was a friend of Joan. They took her home and burried her. Kel did not go. The police told the newspapers that a stray bullet had ended the life of Joan Rydell. Many grieved, but only a few knew of Kel's involvement with her, and no one knew they were married.

Kel immediately moved to another apartment. He stayed there for a week without leaving. His landlady did his shopping for groceries as he told her that he was having trouble walking, and paid her for her effort. He had disappeared. The arms dealers who had tried to assassinate him could not find a trace of him. They had men covering all modes of transportation to no avail.

After a week he left Boston dressed as an old man and left by train for Washington D.C. He arrived mid-morning, and went directly to Stanton's office. Stanton received him immediately. Two of Stanton's aids came in and Kel told of the arm's dealers trying to kill him, and only his girlfriend saved his life, but forfeited hers.

Kel said, "I think the ringleader is Stanton Graves."

Stanton said, "I think we should have the U. S. Marshal in

Boston arrest him. We will keep him isolated, and give him a choice. Either he cooperates with us completely, or we will charge him with murder. That might scare him enough to tell us what we want to know.

"You did a fine job, Kel. You did exactly what we wanted done. Are you ready for another assignment?"

"Not quite, Mr. Stanton. I would like to go home for a couple of weeks. I've some private matters I need to attend to."

"You deserve the time off. I'll expect you back the first of next month. Have a good trip."

He left that evening, as he was informed that a passenger ship was leaving from a port near Richmond going to Houston. It wasn't a large ship, but it had about thirty passengers. It also carried cargo. It was a modern steamship, and had a dining room and a lounge. His cabin was off the main deck. He paid extra to get the best cabin available.

He went to the lounge that evening as he had eaten before he boarded the ship.

A group of people who seemed to be together were having a party. He ordered a brandy, and was about to leave the bar when a gentleman asked if he cared to play in a poker game. Kel had never played poker so he said, "Thank you for inviting me, but I don't play the game. A woman who was standing next to the man said, "Good, you can keep us poker widows from boredom."

He looked at the lady, and she was easy to look at. She was probably in her mid-thirties, and was shapely. She wore expensive jewelry and stylish clothes, which told him that she was of the gentry. He said, "My name is Kelton Keller."

She said, "I'm Katy Norman and I would like it if you called me Katy."

"Then you must call me Kel. Was that your husband?"

"No, I'm a widow. What do you do, Kel?"

"I'm a lawyer by trade, but as of late I have given up my practice to travel."

"Where are you headed?"

"To Austin, Texas. Where are you headed, Katy?"

"A group of us are going to Galveston. We hear the weather is delightful. One of our group has just finished building a resort there, and has invited us to the opening."

"Sounds like fun."

"I'm afraid our group is not very productive, and live an unfruitful life."

"What did your husband do?"

"He was into railroads. Unfortueately, one of his competitors got into an argument with him. That ended in a duel which caused his demise. Walter was older, but a delight to be around. That was well over a year ago, so the sting of his departure is not as prevalent as it used to be."

"I'm sorry. I see you have gotten on with life, which is a compliment to you. I've found that misfortunes should be left in the past."

"Instead of meeting the other ladies, would you take me to the bow to enjoy the salt air?"

"That sounds like a fine idea. I enjoy the salt air, also."

They left and walked in silence until they were at the bow. The sea was calm, but the ship still cut through the water so that a salt spray was left in the air.

Katy broke the silence and said, "Do you have anything you want to accomplish in life?"

"That is a very good question. I haven't really thought about that. I'm glad you asked that question. It's quite provocative, and I must think about that while we are at sea. I find that aboard a ship leaves one time to assess his life. I hope I am able to answer that question before we reach Texas.

"How about you, Katy? What do you wish to accomplish."

"I use to want children, but Walter and I weren't able to accomplish that. I think that is one of the penalties of marrying an older man."

"My, how old was Walter?"

"When I married him he was seventy-two. I didn't realize he was that old as he lived an active life, and was handsome. We were married seven years.

"I was married before to a naval officer. He was gone most of the time. He left on a cruise to Europe, and no word was ever heard from his ship again. I waited seven years, and they declared him dead. It's hard not knowing what happened. The sea seemed to have swallowed him up. I met Walter about a year after that. I knew he was older, but he did all the things a woman likes, and was such a gentleman. I don't think I loved him like my first husband, but he was a delight to be around."

"How about you, Kel. Have you ever been married?"

"I was married to person in show business for a short time, but she left me."

"Yes, temptation is always around people in that trade. I had a cousin who was an actress. She was married three times that I know of, but none lasted very long. She seemed to be looking for something that she could never find."

"It's call happiness."

Katy turned to him and said, "Yes, I suppose it was. I have had happiness, and know what it's like, but never deep happiness."

"How do you know what deep happiness is?"

"A good question, but I will know when it happens."

"I think the deepest love anyone can have, will be when we marry Jesus."

"What an odd statement. You believe Christ will marry us, even the men."

"Yes, because the Bible says so. I think our love for Jesus will supercede sexual love. It will be the love that the Greeks called agape love. They say there are three kinds of love, philo, eros and agape love. Philo is brotherly love, Eros is sexual love and agape love is the love for Christ."

"My you are an interlectural. I think I will stick to Eros love, as I don't understand agape love. Would you explain that to me."

"I think admiration is combined with adoration so deeply that it saturates you. You will want to be next to that person forever."

"You make a woman feel part of that. I don't even know you, but I feel I want to be near you. You make me feel things I have never felt. You're not overly handsome, and seem to be an ordinary man, but spending just the little time I have with you, sends chills up my spine. Will you hold me."

Kel complied and took her in his arms. She laid her head against him and held him tightly. No words were spoken.

Katy just held on. She then said, "I'm beginning to understand agape love. However, there is some eros with it."

They stayed that way until they heard the footsteps of people approaching them, they then stood apart looking at the moon that had just pushed its way throught the clouds.

It was the group of women who Katy described as poker widows. One of the group said, "Katy, I see you dashed off with this handsome man. How selfish of you."

"Margret, after you get to know him, I bet you will try to dash off with him yourself."

"The moonlight can do wonderful things to you, aboard a ship," Margret replied.

"Introduce him to us, Katy."

"This is Kelton Keller, from Austin, Texas, but of late the world. He's now a traveler. These ladies are Margret Schuler, Anne Rhodes and Patty Barron. They are all semi-happily married.

"He's a lawyer by trade, but has since quit fleesing the citizens, and is now spending their money."

Anne said, "Are you in love now, Katy?"

"Yes, I am. And you would be too, if you had just heard him give his description of love. However, I will share him, now. Please give each one of these love-starved women a hug. It won't take you long, and they can then describe a shipboard romance to all who ask."

Kel said, "Maybe they don't want a stranger to hug them."

"Oh, but we do, Kel," and Margret fell into his arms, and stayed there awhile. Then Anne came, then Patty."

"You can't imagine the joy you just gave us," said Margret.

We will blow this up to our friends like it was a torrid romance."

Kel then spoke a latin phrase that he had learned in a latin class in high school. "In English it means, "The love of one to many. That really doesn't express the deeper meaning, but that is as close as I can get in English."

Anne said, "I'm in love."

"We all are, Anne. He just said, the love of one to many," said Patty.

"Seriously, I think Christ will be able to give us more love than we ever felt here on earth, and he can do it at the same time with everyone."

"You mean he will be able to love each of us individually at the same time? There may be millions in heaven."

"The word is omnipresent or ubiquitous. Which means, being with everyone individually at the sametime. The Bible says that no one has ever seen God, so I look at God as the air of the earth, it is around everything on earth all the time. I think God is around, and in everything that is in the universe. I feel we will feel his presence, and his love all the time in heaven. Some people have that now. But most of us will have to wait until we are in heaven.

All the women were in deep thought now. Patty said, "You should have been a minister, Kel. I got more out of your short talk, than all the church services I have attended all my life. Would you consider being a minister?"

"No, I grieve our Lord too much. I have not been called, and I am surely not worthy."

"My what have you done?" asked Margret.

"I don't what to tell you, but it was a dreadful sin that God has forgiven me for, but I have not quite forgiven myself. I should, but I think about it everyday."

"Please tell us, Kel so we can pray for you," asked Anne. "God will hear our prayers and may heal you from this open wound."

"That may help," said Kel. "But if I tell you, you must swear that you will never repeat it to anyone, not even your husbands." They all nodded and Kel said, "I killed four men in gunfights. They were pushed on me every time. However, I could have told them I was a coward, and was afraid. However, my ego caused their death. Had I swallowed my pride those men may have changed their ways, now they have no chance to do that. I sometimes wish they had killed me instead."

All then turned and walked back to their rooms in silence. Katy held onto Kel. They reached her cabin first, and she pulled him around and kissed him. It was a tender kiss.

When Kel was in his bed, he wished he had not told the girls. They so wanted to know, but after learning it, they didn't want to know. He knew each would pray for him, because he saw he had touched each of them. He hoped that they would take his sin and relate it to their own sins. Maybe he had helped each of them.

He then thought of Joan. She always thought her sins were grater than his. He wondered if everyone who loved Christ, thought the same way.

They docked in Galveston, and Kel was asked to come to the resort with the group. It turned out to be a very upscale place that employed a number of people. They even had a place to swim that was very nice. Kel didn't have a swimming suit, but they furnished him a suit that he could wear. The suit came to his knees and his torso was fully clothed. The women wore suits nearly like his, but with some frills on them.

All of the women had shapley bodies, but their husbands all had pot bellies. There were a number of people there, most of which were over fifty. Their host was Gilbert Andrews, who told them about the evening show that was to be put on at eight that night. They would have dinner at tables in front of the stage.

The dinner and the show were great. Kel really enjoyed himself. Katy was near him all the time. He left her at her room and went to bed. The next morning Katy saw him off, even though he left early to catch a boat that was taking a number of people to Houston. As he was leaving Katy handed him an envelope.

She said, "I left you a couple of addresses. Either will reach me. I hope you will write." Kel didn't promise, he just smiled and hugged her goodbye.

He spent the night in Houston near a stage station. He bought a ticket for Austin. It left early the next morning. They stayed in the stage station where he had killed the three men at the nearby saloon. He didn't leave the stage station. The owner didn't recognize him, and even gave him several drinks from his brandy bottle. Two other men were there.

One of the men told about the shooting that had occurred about a year ago. He said, "This man was in the saloon and gunned down three men. They say the men he gunned down were gunmen from Texas, but this was a city dude, dressed somewhat like you," as he indicated Kel.

The man said, "They goaded this man, but he did

everything he could to get out of the fight, but the men in the end drew on him. He shot all three. Only one of them got a shot off and it went into the floor. It made everyone around here a lot more polite than they had been, and no one accosts a stranger, because you never know."

Kel made no comment. He just sipped his brandy.

When he arrived in Austin he went straight to the law firm. Greta was the first person he saw, and she screamed. All came to see what was a matter. He learned that Lorie had married Pat and now only Cindy was left.

Cindy said, "Well, Kel, I guess you're going to have to marry me or I will be an old maid."

Lorie said, "That is a proposal, Kel."

Kel smiled and said, "I'm disappointed that all three of you didn't marry me."

They all came into his arms and Cindy said, "We are all married to you. You just don't sleep with us."

Pat was there and said, "I'm amazed that you didn't sleep with them, Kel. They all love you more that anyone on earth."

Greta said, "Kel loves us beyond sexual love, Pat."

"Thank heavens for that," said Pat, and everyone laughed.

Kel went home and his mother hugged him tightly. Landon came in a half hour later and he hugged him, also.

Kel gave them a bland description of his work for the attorney general, and ended by saying he enjoyed his work. Kel then said, "Greta's husband has planned a dinner dance tonight. Would you like to attend?"

Landon said, "Thank you, but we will just have a quiet evening at home. You young people enjoy yourselves."

Greta's husband had planned the dinner dance at the best place in town. They even had a small band.

As Cindy was dancing with Kel she said, "I want you to marry me, Kel. All the others have mates and I'm all that's left."

"We haven't even kissed Cindy. It may take awhile to become romantic."

"She said, "I'll explain sex to you after the ceremony."

Kel laughed and said, "I've missed you, Cindy. I need to explain some things to you and the girls. I didn't yesterday because of all the business we had to cover. I will consider your proposal, but you know me, I'm slow at commitments."

"I know, I thought I had better ask now, before you turn sixty."

The next day Kel explained that he was a U. S. Marshal at large and worked for the attorney general. He told about his work in Boston, but did not tell them about Joan. He felt this was only his business.

CHAPTER 12

THE TRIP TO THE EAST

Ft. Sumter was fired upon the next day and the war was on. It only took a day before he was called upon by a Texas Ranger. The ranger was Farley Taylor. He said, "I was told by several cowboys that you are one of the best. I want to commission you as a lieutenant in the Texas brigade."

"I am honored, Captain Taylor, but I'm a U. S. Marshal. I will do much more good for the war effort as a U. S. Marshal than with a cavalry company. But thank you."

"You can't do much law enforcement as a U. S. Marshal as your badge will not be honored in Texas. I suggest you see the Governor about being appointed as a Texas Ranger. I just hope you can keep the law while we're gone. They took most of the Texas Rangers for the war effort. I think only fifteen were left for the entire state, and most of them are nearly fifty.

"You may be right, but those fifty-year olds are proably the best lawmen in the country."

"You're right there. I rode with some of them. They are the best."

Kel wired the attorney general and asked for orders. The return wire said, "Return here as you are needed. The U. S.

Marshal that was in San Antonio is now a major with JEB Stuart. If you stay in Texas, you may be arrested as a spy."

Kel immediately took the telegram to the group. They all said that he should leave. Cindy said to the group, "There goes my chance at marrying, Kel."

Lorie said, "He's a hard one to snare, but while he's gone, we will conspire to that end, Cindy."

Going back East by ship was not possible now, so Kel planned to go by stage. The group helped plan this, as all were concerned with his safety. He would go from Austin to Ft. Worth then to Little Rock, and from there to Memphis, Tennessee. He would traverse Tennessee onto Virginia and from there to Washington D.C.

He had enough money as the group had gave him his share of their earnings. He had his shouder holtster that housed his snubnosed thrity-two.

The trip was long and hard. It took two weeks to get to Memphis, Tennessee. Then the trip through Tennessee seemed to take forever. Kel was now in Virginia. At Roanoke, Kel was on a stage headed for Washington D.C. The passengers were a young lady and a middle aged woman. Not much conversation ensued.

They were ten miles out of Roanoke, when they heard shots. The stage came to a stop, and there was another shot. They were in the middle of no where. They could see that six Rebel soldiers had stopped the stage.

One of the Rebels said, "Come on out of that stage." Kel opened the door and stepped out, so he could help the ladies.

One of the Rebels said, "Look at what we have here," as he leered at the women, lasciviously.

The leader said, "Search that dude for weapons. Kel had moved his holter further toward his back, and one of the rebels looked inside his coat and said, "The dude is clean, I had better search the women cause you never know."

As he searched the women he felt their breasts and said, "Nothing but some fine tits."

They led the stage off the trail, and into a small glade. They tied Kel up, and put him against a large rock. Kel noticed the rock had a sharp edge. They picketed their horses, but never unhitched the stagecoach. One of them built a fire, and brought out some cooking utenciles.

The leader said, "You women fix us some vitals. One of the men had taken a large pack off their packhorse, and dropped it by the fire. A stream ran close to the fire. The younger woman took a pot, and retrieved some water, while the older one opened the pack, and found some side meat and cans of beans. She took one of the pots and a frying pan, and put them on some rocks near the fire, and began to fry beacon.

Kel could see the Rebels had killed the driver, and the man riding shotgun. They were now going through their pockets, and searching the coach for a strong box.

After they were finished with the coach, one of the Rebels was left to guard Kel. They were about fifty feet from the fire. Kel could smell dinner was being cooked. The men did not offer the girls anything to eat until they were finished. One of them carried a tray for the man who was guarding Kel. When they were through eating they handed the women their trays and the women ate from their trays as they were starved.

There was coffee, and one of the Rebels produced a

whiskey bottle that they poured in with their coffee. It was dark now, but the men had brought wood, and had a blazing fire. As they drank the leader said, "I would like to see you girls dance for us."

"There is no music," the older woman said.

"Then sing as you dance."

"Another man said, "It would be better if they danced naked."

"Yeah! the other's said.

One of the men near the younger woman took his hand, and that he put just below her neck. He then ripped straight down, and her dress fell off of her. She was now standing in her underwear. One of the others said, "Are you going to take it off or shall I take it off."

She then began to undo the underwear. The older woman undressed without saying anything. Kel could hear everything as could his guard. His guard left Kel and went to watch the women dance.

The minute the guard left, Kel moved his body toward the sharp edge of the rock. He was up against it now, and started rubbing his wrists up and down as fast as he could to cut the ropes.

The women dance for a minute or so when one of the men took down his pants and jumped the young woman who was dancing with her eyes closed. The minute she hit the ground two of the men held her while the other raped her.

The older woman had been taken down, and while two of the men held her the other raped her. When he was through, he moved to holding her, and another was on her.

Kel now had his wrists free, and he was working on his

feet. It took him awhile, but now he was ready. He checked his gun, then moved toward the men. The men were too engrossed in their activity, and didn't see Kel step within ten feet of them. He shot the two men who were on top of the women. The other men had their pistols under their clothes that were down to their ankles, and as they searched for them, Kel shot all four of them. He then walked up, picked up one of the pistols, and shot each of the men again in the head.

The women were standing now. Kel said, "Go to the stage, and find your bags. You can redress with the clothes in your bags. You may want to bathe in the creek before you dress."

While the women were gone, Kel thought, *"This is just a patrol. The main body will be looking for them come mid-morning. I could strip the men and scalp them as if Indians killed them."* He went to his work stripping the men. He found a sharp knife on one of the bodies. After they were stripped, he scalped them. It was a gruesome job, but one that had to be done.

He put the scalps in one of the shirts and tied it up. He put another shirt around it so it didn't show blood. He mixed his package with the clothes. He then went to the creek to wash his hands. The women were now at the stagecoach redressing. He then went to the stage and the women had just finished dressing.

He said, "It's light enough to keep on the trail. As soon as I water the horses we will travel. I want you both to ride up with me. The women liked this idea as they wanted to be close to Kel.

The women helped as they watered all the horses. Kel used the ropes on the saddles to tie each of the Rebel's horses to the back of the stage. They took the packs from the packhorse and put them inside the stage. The women had not said a word. While they were traveling, Kel asked, "Do you women know one another?"

The older woman said, "We just met on the stage."

Kel said, "Good. No one will ever know what happened here but we three. I advise you each to never mention this to anyone. No one will ever know but you. Just take it as part of life. It happened, and now it's over. I hope it won't scar your lives. I killed those six men. I took everything they had in life and everything they would have had. I will have to live with that. I think killing a man is much worse than being raped. You had no choice, but then I didn't either. We all must put this behind us. Do you think you can do it?"

The younger said, "It will take time. Another thing is that we both might be pregnant. That will be hard to explain to my fiance."

"Marry him as quickly as you can, and you will never know if it's his child or one of the rapers. However, you can love that child like no other, as it has a bond with you."

The older woman said, "I don't think I can have a child, but I'm married, and will sleep with my husband as soon as I can." She then looked at the younger woman and said, "I think we are covered, Mary. If we do have a child, let's name him Kel if it's a boy and Kelly if it's a girl."

"I will surely do that Kay. Kel, we can never repay you for what you did. We may never meet again, but we will pray for you the rest of our lives."

Kel smiled and said, "I will pray for you, also. When we meet in heaven, we will have a joyful reunion."

They had somehow missed the trail to the way station. Although they missed a night's sleep they traveled until dark. They found an abandoned farmhouse at dusk and pulled up to that. It had a pump outside and a dry watering trough for the horses.

The pump wouldn't work without priming. They serched the house for any liquid to prime the pump, but found only a half gallon of vinegar. Kel poured it into an iron pail then looked at the women and said, "You both need to contribute to the liquid in this bucket for me to prime the pump. They took the bucket into a bedroom, and did their chore. Kel added to the liquid himself. With what he had, he prayed that it was enough to priime the pump. It worked and water flowed. He filled the trough first, then rinsed the pail and brought a bucket of fresh water to the house. While he was doing that the women brought the packs into the house and built a fire in the fireplace. They began to cook supper. Kel made coffee when he came in. He took the rebel's whiskey and poured it into their coffee and said, "This will settle us down."

Before going to bed, Kel found some hay and fed the animals. They were tied next to the watering trough so they had plenty of water. He then took the men's clothing along with the scalps and burned them. He added wood, so all the cloth burned along with the scalps.

They made pallets, and were soon asleep. They woke early and after a breakfast, were on their way. It began to rain, so Kel pulled up, and they all got into the coach and napped. It was just a squall, and soon passed.

They reached Lynchburg, and found that it was in Rebels

hands. Kel drove to the livery stable, and sold the Rebel's horses. He divided the money with the women. They decided to just keep the coach and drive on. They stayed in a hotel that night, and all had a bath and a good meal.

Kay said, "I don't feel safe without you, Kel. Get a room with two double beds. Mary and I will sleep together, and you will be in the bed beside us."

Mary said, "I feel the same, Kel. Just tell the clerk we're your sisters."

They slept late, but were on the road by ten that morning. They traveled through small towns and always stayed in hotels. Kay said, I was headed for Richmond, so I had better get out at the next place that they provide travel to Richmond. You two can go on to Washington if they will let you through the lines."

Kay left them and they traveled on. They came to road block, but after convincing the guards that they were no threat to the war, were let through. They were also stopped again by the Union army, and were let through when Kel showed his U. S. Marshal badge.

Kel drove Kay to where her parents were to meet her. She hugged him and said, "I will never forget you, Kel. Goodbye."

Kel drove the coach to a livery stable, and asked the hostler to feed the animals and to store the coach.

He then went to his apartment, took a bath and changed clothes. He soaked in the tub, and thought of the women that had been in his life. Joan had really loved him, but he thought most of her love was sexual. She wanted him every night, and it was really more than he wanted. However, he did his best to please her.

Katy loved him and knew if he wrote her, she would want to be involved with him. He then thought of Cindy. Although he loved her, she was like a sister, and it would be hard to become romantically involved with her. He thought she could do that a lot easier than he could.

He knew he wanted a woman in his life, but he just hadn't met her. Maybe he should marry Cindy. She wanted and needed him.

He thought of how life would be with her. He had no sexual love for her, and that would be hard to overcome. He then thought he may do it for Cindy's sake. He just didn't know.

CHAPTER 13

A NEW ADVENTURE

At the attorney general's office he was shown into Stanton's office. He was met by a new attorney general. Stanton had been named as the secretary of war, and Edward Bates was the new attorney general.

Bates said, "Ed said, you would be calling. He wants you to go to his office. He asked me to keep you on as a U. S. Marshal at large. After hearing him tell of your exploits, I agreed that you should keep your badge, as I will need you from time to time.

Kel called on Stanton, and Stanton was pleased to see him. He said, "A lot has happened since we last met. I guess you heard about the fiasco at Manassis. General Winfield Scott and his field commander General McDowell were going to Richmond to end the war. However, the Southern Army met them at Bull Run and gave them a sound beating.

"Since then there has been two generals try to take Richmond, both failing. The last one at Seven Pines, they were severly beaten, again. We were then all afraid that General Lee would take Washington.

"The president has now appointed General McClellan.

The men of the army like him and he seems to be what Lincoln wants. However, we need someone with McClellan so we have an inside look as well as an outside look of his leadership.

"I understand he has taken his troops to Maryland to regroup. I have talked with President Linclon at length as we meet daily. I advised the President that we need someone on General McClellan's staff who can keep us up to date on his strategy. That someone is you, Kel."

"What do I know about military strategies? I've never been in the army."

"We don't want a military man, we want someone who has a decerning mind that can assess what is happening in each engagement. You have an excellent mind, and can give us that.

"After telling the president about you, he agreed that you are the one he wants. If you agree, we will set you up in the historical agency, and tell McClellan that we want you on his staff to record the war. This will provide your cover. You will be given the military rank of major. We now need to see the president. He is expecting us."

At the president's office, Lincoln remembered Kel's piano playing, and remarked how he enjoyed it. He said, "I had no idea that you were the same fellow that Ed was telling me about. I am well pleased with your selection, Ed."

Kel said, "Thank you, Mr. President. I know how vital the information you want is to you and Secretary Stanton. I will do my best."

"We want you to become friends with the general, and win his confidence. He's a likable fellow, and the men in his army adore him. You are to leave as soon as we can brief you of what we're looking for and arrange your military status.

"I will meet you occasionally as the mail is probably monitored. Ed thought of a plan where we can meet face to face. He suggested that we have a woman pose as your sweetheart. You can tell General McClellen that you need to meet with her at least twice a month or you may lose her. I will go with this woman as her chaperone dressed as a woman."

"I have the perfect girl to play that role, Mr. President. I've known her since the first day I entered college. We are partners in a law firm in Austin. We have never been envolved romantically. However, the other two girls in our firm are now married and Cindy suggested that we marry the last time we were together. As I always looked at her like I would a sister, it was hard for me to think of her that way, however, I told her I would think about it. She is brilliant, and about my age. Her name is Cindy Newhart."

Stanton said, "We could have a ship pick her up and bring her here. We still have places in Texas that would be safe for that."

"Get it done." Lincoln smiled and said, "You had better go with the ship, Major Keller."

Kel smiled at his new title and said, "I will, Mr. President." Arrangements were made and three weeks later Kel arrived in Austin. He went straight to the law firm and entered. Cindy was the first to see him and she was shocked. She said, "Why are you here, Kel?"

"Get the girls, we need to talk."

At the meeting Kel thoroughly explained his new job. He

said, "We have selected you to be my girlfriend, Cindy. I told the president that no one could play that roll as well as you."

Cindy said, "I like using the war as a prop to get you to marry me. The group met and all agreed that our marriage was for the good of the group."

Kel smiled and said, "It may take me awhile, but I guess it has been decided. In our meetings there will be the element of truth. The Bible says that the truth will make you free, but it is doing the opposite in this case," and they all laughed.

Kel added, "Please keep this as a secret that only the group is privileged to."

They left the next day and were in Washington ten days later. They went straight to Stanton's office and he went personally to show Cindy her new apartment, and then took her to her job. It was a historical government agency, and they had been briefed that a new staff member was coming aboard to cover the war.

After she was shown to her office, they then went to the white house and met with President Lincoln. They talked about how they would communicate to when and where meetings would be made. When the president wanted to meet with Kel he would have Cindy write Kel a letter telling him where and when to meet her.

A Colonel Williams was a close confidemt of the presidents, and he was to escort Kel to meet with General McClellan.

McClellan met Kel with a jauntiest eye. He said, "You aren't a spy are you?"

Kel said, "I am only here to record the battles, and aide you the best I can, General. Please use me as you would any other of your staff. I will keep from being underfoot, and will aide you in anyway, I can."

"Well, your writing won't take that much time, so I will use you. Right now my staff and I are not receiving things we need. You can greatly aide me by getting that done."

"Please have your staff write out in detail what they need, and I will see that it is furnished as quickly as I possible can."

McClellan turned to Colonel Williams and said, "Bill, I already like this guy. I just wish everyone who served under me, had his attitude. Tell the President he sent the right man."

Kel had gotten off on a good foot, and he made good on his promise. Of course the president's staff saw he got everything he asked for.

One evening only MeClellan and Kel were in the general's office, and he brought out a bottle brandy. He poured Kel a snifter and said, "Tell me about yourself, Kel."

Kel used this opportunity to tell McClellan about Cindy. He did it with such passion that McClellan could feel Kel was in love."

"Well, Kel, let's not let this war get in the way of a romance. While you were talking, it brought back memories of my wife and our first days together. I couldn't wait to see her, and I see you feel the same way about Cindy. I will do my best to let you see her as often as the war allows. The two months we have been together, I see the value of your service to me."

Kel had resolved that even though he really liked McClellan, he would tell Linclon the bare truth of what he observed with McClellan.

Cindy wrote just after the battle of Antietam. Lincoln had left the white house by a basement door and walked three blocks to a barn where a carriage awaited him. He was dressed as an older woman with a scarf around his face and a large woman's hat. They traveled to a small village about halfway between where McClellan had withdrawn his troops to, and Washington D.C.

The village had a hotel, and they went directly to the rooms Kel had rented. Cindy went into Kel's arms and Lincoln said, "I can see that we used the right woman, Kel."

They sat, and Kel had coffee for them. Kel sat on a couch with Cindy beside him. He said, "Lee pulled his troops away from the battle. I think his supplies had run thin. I think McClellan could have pressed him and won the battle, but as before he withdrew his troops.

"I asked him why didn't he pursue Lee, and he said that his troops needed to rest and regroup. I think he missed a golden opportunity."

"I would have never known that, but for you, Kel. We had nearly twice the troops as Lee, but instead of a victory, it was a draw. That will give Lee time to regroup and take it to us again.

"I will leave you two as I need to get some rest. I have been up all night."

When Lincoln and his aide were gone, Cindy said, "Do I have a chance, Kel?"

"You do, Cindy. There is no one in this world I love more. It will take me awhile to discard my brotherly instincts I think. But if we keep meeting, and I get those flowing love letters, I can see it happening. After all I would never disappoint the group."

Cindy said, "At least I have that going for me. Do you ever think of having children?"

"No, it has never crossed my mind. However, I will start thinking about that. The thought of children brings mixed emotions to me. I have so much to accomplish, and they would surely be underfoot now, but later if we have a house in Austin, I can see having a few."

"Just think, you can teach them the truths of Jesus and make missionaries out of them. Maybe not the ones who go to Africa, but among there own friends. I think that is where missionaries are needed the most. I know you really changed the groups spirituality. We saw what Jesus did a lot clearer. Just think of what you can do with our children."

"Our children. That surely puts a different light on our relationship. I want to love you so much I can't bear to be without you. I will pray that the Lord spread his mantle on both of us, until we are saturated with love."

"Kel you have such a way of expressing your thoughts that the person you are talking to understands the utmost of what you're saying. You should write. Yes, that should be your aspiration in life. I so love you. I want more though. As you said, 'I want to be so inlove that I cannot bear to be without you.'"

"Well, meeting you today has started my thinking aknew. Children, our children, that has a nice sound to it. I bet you will be a wonderful mother. I want our family to be close with Jesus at the center of it. I want us to instill in our children a love for Christ that passes all understanding. If we are very careful, I think we can do that.

"Of couse there is this dreadful war. It seems neither side has an advantage. The North has many more men and supplies, but the South has much the superior leadership. That "Stonewall" Jackson tricks us every time. If he were on the North's side, this war would already be over."

The war dragged on as McClellan was overly cautious. It didn't take Kel's briefing for Lincoln to see his hesitations. Lincoln replaced McClellan some weeks later. He re-assigned him to Washington D.C., but never gave him another assignment. McClellan had formed an attachment to Kel, and asked him to stay with him as his aide."

Kel said, "My assignment is to cronical the war and I can't do that from Washington D.C."

"But you can aid me. They can get someone else to write about the war."

"I'll have to check with my boss. Then I'll let you know."

Lincoln said, "Your assignment is to watch McClellan. I have heard he has political asspirations. I think it would be best to stay with him and keep me informed."

When Kel returned he said, "My boss assigned another man to cover the war. He said that my duty to you supercedes my writing."

McClellan was well pleased. He put in for Kel's rank to be raised to a light colonel. When Lincoln learned of this he smiled and said, "You are doing a great job, Kel. If I'm reelected, I might put you on my staff."

Now that Kel was in the city, he met with Cindy every night. He loved her, but could never get to the point that he was in love with her. He thought that seeing her on a daily basis may bring her closer to him. He tried to envision sexual relations with her and thought it almost incestuous. He finally concluded it would take some time.

CHAPTER 14

A CHANCE IN TIME

McClellan resigned his commission after he was nominated to run as the Democrat nominee for president. He ran on a promise to sue for peace with the South to end the war. Many were for this, as many had lost sons, husbands and sweethearts in the war. The war was becoming very unpopular. Lincoln knew he must have victories. He had promoted Grant to head the army. This infuriated many generals in the army as Grant went around nineteen generals to assume that post.

Lincoln saw Grant as a winner, and he knew he must have a string of victories to win the election. Lincoln instructed Grant to press the enemy at all costs. It was costly as Grant obeyed his instruction. The North had back to back victories at Gettysburg and Vicksburg. It was enough to swing the election of 1864.

True to his word, Lincoln invited Kel to be one of his advisors. Trouble was brewing out west. The Sioux, at the urging of Red Cloud, had assemble thousands of Indians. Many of which had been lifetime enemies. Red Cloud had a gift of persuasion and met with various tribes of the Indiana nations. They all saw the invasion by the whitemen coming into their hunting grounds, and destroying their way of life. They had killed nearly half the buffalo and polluted the streams and cut the forest. They had to be stopped, so feuding between themselves stopped, and most of the tribes came to aid the Sioux.

They were now slaughtering villages and wagon trains. They had overrun forts and slaughtered collums of soldiers.

Lincoln had sent General Carrington and several others to put down the Indians, but still reports came in about the unrest. It seemed they could not stop the Indians. Lincoln called in Kel and said, "I must have an unbiased opinion of why the army cannot contain the Indians. I view you as a person who can make a wise assessment. I would like you to go out West and find out why our army is unable to bring the Indians in check. Will you do that for me?"

"Of course, Mr. President. I will need to study where our troops are, the number of them, what armorment and supplies they have. Then I must know nearly the same thing about the Indians.

"I can get the information of our army here in D.C., but I must assess the Indians in the field. I know you cannot spare more troops as this time, but as soon as the war is over you will have to assign more troops to stop the Indians."

Kel spent a week checking the armies of the West and their supplies. He then engaged a scout that was now in Washington as he had led a group of men from the New Mexico territory, mostly Hispanic, since 1862 to fight in the war. Kel talked to Lincoln about him and he was assigned to Kel for the mission.

His name was Kit Carson, and he was a seasoned mountain man. He knew the West better than anyone. Kel spent hours going over what they were to achieve.

Carson said, "The problem is not an easy one to solve. Red Cloud now has every Indian thinking like he does. They are fighting for their country like we are fighting for ours. You have to understand that the Indians were here first and now we are taking their land from them."

"That does put this war in a different prospective. However, the Indian does not kow the tactics of war. Our men have the best arms and have been trained to fight."

"Fighting an Indian is much different than the fighting our men have been trained to do. The Indians are probably the best light cavalry in world. An Indian can ride for days without sleep. They will ride their horse to death, then eat him and look for another. Their horses are mustangs. They are much lighter and faster than the horses we brought from the East. An Indian can survive on very little water, and knows where all the water in the desert is located. They lay traps that our soldiers have no knowledge of. In short they are much the more skilled in their own land.

"The only thing we have going for us is that we have more men and have rifles that they don't. They have captured a number of rifles and ammunition, but still depend on their bows and arrows. Every Indian tribe has their own leader, and their ego won't let anyone supersede their own leader.

"Indians will be peaceful one day and trade with the whites, and the next day slaughter a wagon train. They are whimsical people. You never know from day to day what they will do."

"I will put all you said in my report, Kit. You are probably the formost authority of the Indians in America. I will put your name behind all your statements so the President will know it comes from the best authority."

"Well, I'm not the best. The best is Jim Bridger, and he's where he needs to be and that's with Carrington. I understand that Carrington has built a new fort beyond fort Laramie. It's called Fort Kearney. Carrington is an engineer. I'm told he laid out a splendid fortress as only he could do. We need to go to Fort Kearney as Bridger is there, and can give us exactly what is needed, and what the situation is. I trust him more than any other man."

The week before he left Kel spent his evenings with Cindy. She asked, "When are we to be married, Kel?"

"I will think about that on my trip out West." He had already explained to her that the president was dispatching him to the West to make an evaluation of the Indian situation, and didn't know how long that would take.

Kel said, "I think we will be married, but I must be sure. I know you would make a great wife and a wonderful mother. I just have to assess myself as I am not sure of myself. You want a husband that loves you deeply, and I need to know if I can do that." He kissed her goodbye and departed.

They took a train to Chicago. Carson said, "We can't go from Chicago directly to Cheyenne. The Indians now control the area in between. Two men traveling alone would only be lucky if they crossed that land without losing their scalps. I have many friends with the Indians, but that will do us no good, as they now see me as their emeny. I suggest we take a the train to Alton, the town just outside St. Louis. The river separates Alton from St. Louis. I know a man there who sells canoes. He trades with the Indians who build these canoes. They are the best. They are light and strong. They are long enough to carry our trappings and food, but still narrow enough to paddle upstream at a fast rate.

"We will go up the Missouri River until it intersects the Platt River. We will then travel the Platt at night, and if we are lucky, go around the Sioux. The Missouri would normally be dangerous, but there has been considerable sickness with the Indians there. A small pox epidemic and chlora have decimated the tribes, so we can travel the river and have little resistance.

"When we reach the Platt, we will travel at night, and as silently as possible. We will sleep during the daytime. I know many hiding places, and we should be safe."

They reached Alton and just as Kit had said, they met John Chapman who had a fine canoe for them. They paid too much, but Carson said, "I want Chapman to make money so he will stay in business. He does a great service for us mountain men."

"Before we depart, I would like to know if you believe in Jesus Christ?"

Kit smiled and said, "I would not step foot in that canoe if I didn't."

"Then let me bless our canoe and our trip." He raised his arms with his palms out. He noticed that several men around them took off their hats and bowed their heads. This warmed his heart.

He said, "Lord of all the universe and savior of your people, I ask your blessings on our trip. You have saved our nation from being separated. We are all grateful for the Constitution which I believe you inspired as we are one nation under God, indivisible, only because of you. Let Kit's and my trip honor you. Give us your divine wisdom and guidance, and let it serve both the Indians and our country. I ask this in the holy name of Jesus." With that they entered the canoe, and they shoved off.

At places, the Missouri River was difficult to paddle with its swiftness, but other areas were easy, so it all balanced out. The first few days, Kel's shoulders ached at night. But he was able to keep up. He marveled at Carson, who was around fifty years of age. He seemed as storng as a twenty-five year old. Kel prayed at night about his and Cindy's relationship, but said, "Your will be done."

They were now on the Platt River, and they paddled at night and slept during the day. Carson knew places to hole up during the day. Several caves that were on the banks of ther river were inaccessible to anyone on the banks of the river. The caves were dark and cool and they slept very well. They traveled from dusk to dawn.

Kel was amazed at how tasty Carson made the beans that he added herbs and hot peppers to. Carson had traps that he would set during the day, and they most always had meat with their beans.

They stopped at an Arapaho village where Carson had lived at times. The chief especially liked Carson. However, as they walked through the village a young white girl of about six or seven came running to Kel, yelling "Daddy, Daddy!" She grabbed Kels leg and clung to it.

A large warrior stood and shouted something. Kel asked Carson, "What did he say to me?"

"He just challenged you to a fight to the death. That is Oulonisora. You can't get out of this one, Kel. He's the best shot with a rifle in the Indian nation. He's quick and accurate."

"Tell him he can use his rifle and I will use my handgun."

"He will kill you, Kel."

"Maybe, but tell him just the same."

Carson told Oulonisora something in the Indian language which made Oulonisora smile. The chief had heard what was said, and set up the challenge. They stood about fifty feet apart with Oulonisora with his rifle almost pointing at Kel. Kel had his handgun although in its scabbard.

Carson said, "The chief will raise his hand, then bring it down. When he does this, you must draw. Don't anticipate the signal or they will kill you."

Kel looked intently at the chief's hand. It came down sharply and Oulonisora was quick with his rifle, but as he tried to pull the trigger he found he couldn't because a lead bullet was in his heart. He dropped to his knees with a questioning look on his face, then fell forward onto his face, dead.

The little girl ran to Kel and yelled, "You did it Daddy!" She clutched Kel's leg and wouldn't let go.

Carson said, "Do you know this girl?"

Kel said no, but she knows I'm her daddy, so I shall be."

The chief came over and said something to Carson. Carson smiled and said, "You not only won the little girl, but also his two wives. You will stay with them tonight in Oulonisora's tepee, which is now yours.

Carson stayed with Kel and his new family. The little girl pulled Kel over to the tepee where two women stood. One was Indian, but the other was a white woman. Kel asked the white woman, "What is your name. "My name before I was captured was Kathryn Lister. Oulonisora killed my husband and my children, then took me as his wife. I have lived with him for over a year.

Carson ssaid, "We will have to take both women and the child with us when we leave. We can sell them at the next village we come to."

"No, the girl and the white woman will come with us. We will need another canoe, can you arrange for one?"

"Yes, but it will cost you."

"Maybe you can trade the Indian woman for a canoe. That way she can stay with her people."

"A smart idea. I'll do what I can." He then left.

"Kel turned to the little girl and said, "Go gather wood for tonight." She left immediately and Kel took the woman inside the tepee, and motioned for her to sit down. He then said, "What is your name, again?"

She said, "Kathryn Lister."

So tell me Mrs. Lister about what happened to you and the girl."

"About a year ago, our village was attacked by over a hundred Indians. My husband and two children were in to buy supplies when the attack commenced. I could see Paula, the girl here, and her parents being attacked. Oulonisora killed both her parents, but Paula was looking at some other atrocity, and did not see here parents shot. Oulonisora then turn to us. He had a rifle, and killed my husband and two children. He then caught Paula's hand, and brought her to me and said, 'Take.' I gathered that I was to take care of Paula. We were taken with the Indians. Other white women were taken and a few children. They have since been traded to other tribes.

Oulonisora had no children, and liked Paula and me, and would not trade for us. We began living with him. Paula's father looked very much like you. Paula didn't see her father or mother die, so she assumes you are her father who came for her."

Kel said, "Just let her think that. She is euphoric now, and I don't want her to ever be sad again."

"Will you trade me like you're doing with Lucidia?"

"No. You will go with Carson and myself."

"Am I to be your woman?"

"No, you will be your own woman. You are free."

"I am not free. No white man or woman will have anything to do witth me, now that I have lived with an Indian man. Besides I have no money, and no way of supporting myself."

"No one will know you lived with an Indian man, as I am taking you back East."

"I do not read or write. No one will accept me."

"I will, and I shall see that you and Paula are educated so you can once again take your place in society."

"Society, no one will have anything to do with me."

"I will, and so will my friends. I am going to see you have a good life from this point on. Do you know Jesus?"

"Yes, I prayed every night to be rescued. I believe God heard my prayers, and sent you. I loved my husband and will try to love you."

"I am not going to be your husband, as I have a woman who I'm thinking of marrying."

"She will leave you when she sees Paula and me living with you. She will never understand you taking us in and supporting us."

"We will cross that bridge when we come to it. Does Paula call you mother?"

"No, she calls me by my Indian name."

"Tell Paula to call you Kathyrn as I shall do. You are to call me Kel. Paula shall call me daddy. When she is older, I will explain our relationship, but by then, I'll be her daddy."

"You are a kind man, Kel, but then Jesus sent you, so you would be."

Carson returned and said, "I was able to trade the Indian woman for a canoe. The Indian woman liked it, so everyone is pleased."

They left the next day. Carson and Kathryn in one canoe and Kel and Paula in the other. They traveled as they had in the past as the Indians were more hostile as they proceeded up the Platt River to Ft. Laramie. They traveled only at night and slept during the day.

They finally reached Fort Larime. Colonel William Collins received them. Kel handed him the orders that were signed by President Lincoln.

Collins looked up and said, "They don't think I can do this job?"

"That is not at all why we are here. We are here to assess the resourses of the Indians and make recommendation of what it will take to contain them. This is just a stop, we are going on to Fort Kearney."

"Well, Red Cloud is said to have thousands of warriors that he has persuaded that the white men are taking their land. Red Cloud said that the white men broke the 1851 and 1856 treaties. Those treaties proportioned off the lands, and set boundaries for each tribe. The Indians don't even know what a boundary is. Washington's leaders had nine chiefs sign the agreement. These chiefs had no authority over anything, but their own tribe if that. The other Indians laughed at this. These tribes are scattered from Idaho to Missoui, but they are here, and Red Cloud has a way of gathering the amount warriors he needs for any area he wishes to attack.

"They fight a different way. They never stand and fight. They are always on the move. They hit the rear of us, and kill what they can and move away. It's always a few here and few there. They never fight face to face, unless it's an ambush where they have the advantage of the terrain and the number of men.

"They now have rifles and handguns as they have captured countless arms and amuntion. The only advantage we have is our cannons. Well placed cannons do disrupt them. The only reason any fort is still standing is because of the cannons. If they made a frontal attack we would cut them to pieces, and they know it. So, they never make a frontal attack.

"They are well led and know what they're doing. I think they plan to run us all out of the West, and that's what they're doing so far. The only safe places are the forts and the forts are two hundred miles apart, too far to keep people safe. We have told the settlers, but they just keep coming and the Indians just keep killing them.

"Miners are just as bad. For every four miners who come,

Red Cloud kills three of the four, but the greedy bastards just keep coming. Until we can have enough men in the field, it's like murder to send out patrols. And I ask you, patrols to do what? We know they are out there, but in such small groups we can't find them."

"Your assessment is exactly why we are here. You have witten a lot of my report, and I will give you the credit. I will be sure and tell President Lincoln and Secretary Stanton about you, Colonel Collins. I think it will help you be promoted."

"Thank you Colonel Keller, but I'm hoping to do something else in two more years. I want to spend the rest of my life doing the things I always wanted to do, like fishing and hunting and chasing Mrs. Collins around the bedroom." This brought smiles to Kel's and Carson's faces."

"Well, for what it's worth, Colonel, we really appreciated what you said. It just reinforces what Kit said about the Indians. He also said that this is their land and we are the invaders, that alone will bring fright to anyone."

"Let's have a drink, gentlemen. That's about all I can do now. By the way, who is the woman and child you brought with you."

Kit said, "Kel picked them up at an Indian village. Seems an Indian took a dislike to Kel and challenged him to mortal combat. His rifle against Kel's handgun. He had no idea he was up against the fastest gun in the West. I've never seen anyone who could draw as fast and as accurate as Kel. The man he killed is the Arapaho, named Oulonisora."

"Yes, I have heard of him. You must be good, Colonel."

"Please don't tell anyone about that, I hate to kill men. In this case I was fighting for the woman and little girl, and had no choice. I seem to always say that after I have killed someone. I'm a Christian and hate it when I kill. It just seems God places me in places I can do no other."

"My lord, how many have you killed?"

"Oulonisora made eleven. I am surely not proud of it. I ended lives of men who had mothers and fathers who loved them. It's a terrible business."

"Yes, I see what you mean. When I order men into the field, I often send some to their death. I too, carry the same burden."

"I will pray for you, Colonel Collins. I think the most powerful tool on earth is our prayers."

"I'll pray for you too, Colonel. We share a common bond now. I shall never forget this night."

That night Kathryn and Paula stayed with Kel and Kit. Paula came into Kels bed, put her arms around him, and was asleep immediately with the security of her daddy.

They stayed a week interviewing several of the officers and men. They received about the same message as what Colonel Collins gave them. They then started for Fort Kearney. The mail detail and supplies were escorted by a hundred and twenty troopers. As it was winter, the Sioux were up north in their winter lodges.

The covered the hundred and fifty plus miles in six days and were greeted by Colonel Carrington. He was a small man of few words, but had a wife, Margret, who made them feel comfortable. After explaining Kathryn and Paula to her she said, "I'll keep them with us."

Paula said, "Thank you, but I won't be separated from my daddy."

Kit was there and explained the traumatic duel that Kel fought for his daughter. Margret then said, "I understand, Paula, I will just take Kathryn from you."

Kit asked where "Old Gabe," Jim Bridger, was. Carrington asked an orderly to fetch Mr. Bridger. In a few minutes, Bridger came into the room. He and Kit clasped hands and looked deeply into each others eyes. It was obvious the respect each had for the other.

Kel said, "Mr. Bridger, I would like to talk with you when you have time."

Bridger smiled and said, "I'm not used to being called Mr. Bridger unless I'm in trouble."

"If you would you prefer, I will call you, Jim, but if I do, you must call me Kel. Now Carrington did not like familiarity with people who he deemed below officer ranking, and it shown on his face. Kel caught the subtlety.

Later that evening, just Kit and Kel talked with Carrington. Kel explained his mission. Here, Carrington had a lot to say.

He said, "I am stripped to the bone of officers and competent troops. Just to send out the wood detail requires two companies of men to escort them. However, they have nothing else to do. I will not send out patrols as we know the Indians keep watch on us. They seem to know what we are about at every turn. If we did not have the Howitzers they would have already overrun the fort.

"The Bozeman trail is essentially closed. Of course wagon trains still try to go up it, but few make it. I estimate that Red Cloud has over two thousand warriors, and each know how to fight. Red Cloud has the best reconnaissance of any army in America. He is a genius at strategy, and employs his troops as well as any general in the world. I don't see us defeating him unless Grant sends me the men I need. Until then the Bozeman trail should be called the Bloody Trail."

Kel said, "Thank you Colonel Carrington. You have written my report for me. I hope I can quote every word you said to the president. I am also going to talk with Mr. Bridger."

"Now he may have a different view, but I don't think so. I trust that man. He is cautious when he needs to be, and I listen to him. He's the finest scout out here. He's sympathetic to the Indians at times as he has lived with them, and has an Indian wife. Margret treats her as an equal, but then that's my Margret. I couldn't stand it here without her. She's as valuable as Old Gabe."

After talking to Jim Bridger, he said much the same as Carrington. Kel had his report. Kit took them as far as St. Louis, but left them there.

In St. Louis, Kel wanted to buy the girls clothes, and he spent a day with them. He had their hair fixed, and they looked classy. He also took them to a stage show and feed them well.

They took the train back to Chicago and then on to New York City where they spent a day sightseeing. Paula never left his side and slept with him each night. Kathryn thought it was nice that Kel had taken to the girl.

They arrived, and gave their report to Secretary Stanton and the President at the same time.

Kel said, "What I have gathered from both Carson and the officers in the field is that there are over a hundred different tribes. Each tribe is fiercely independent. Each tribe has a leader, but some only have a limited power over his braves. However, Red Cloud is a brilliant diplomat, and has convinced even his enemies that they must band together if they are to defeat the white man's expansion into their land.

"He has essentially closed the Bozeman Trail. They all now look to Red Cloud to lead them. He has told them that the white man is taking their hunting grounds, and will soon run them off their lands unless they fight together.

"They do fight, but not like we whites do. Their's is a guerrilla warfare of hit and run. They are very skilled at this. Small groups of whites are singled out and slaughtered. Carrington described Red Cloud as a military genius. He employs a surveillance system second to none.

"Carrington is a competent leader, and constructed one of the finest Forts I've ever seen. As long as he has his howitzers, he could hold off ten thousand Sioux.

"The Indians way of life has gone on for a thousand years or more, and would continue if the white man had not intervened."

"An excellent report, Kel. I see the situation very clearly now. We will have to finish this war before we can take care of that situation. At least I know what to do now."

After Stanton left, Kel met with President Lincoln alone. He said, "I really hate to tell you this option of putting the Indians away for good. However, after studying their way of life, I feel I must. The Indians live a barbaric lifestyle. They treat their wives like slaves and live only to fight with another tribe. There way of life has brought me to tell you how to end their culture for good."

Kel had Lincoln's attention now. He said, "The Indian's

now live off the land. Because of the large number of Indians in a concentrated area, the buffalo is their chief source of food. If the buffalo are killed off, it will do two things. One, they would be starved into going onto reservations or go back to where they came from, and two, with the departure of the other tribes, the land then could be plowed by the tens of thousands of white people looking to farm it.

"The second solution is to take away their horses. Without horses they cannot survive as the game is two scattered. So, without a food supply and no mobility, they can do none other than live on the reservations.

"The white people think of them as subhuman. Most hate the Indian, and would never take them into their society."

"A cruel solution, but the only practical one," said Lincoln. Thanks for that information. I will probably put it to use."

Kel had to rent a larger place to accommodate Kathryn and Paula. He also convinced Paula that she had to room with Kathryn, now, as it was not proper for her to sleep with him. She couldn't see why, but being Kel said it, she did it without question.

After they were settled, Kel called on Cindy. She was glad to see him, and asked him to tell her about the trip. She was shocked that Kel had brought back the two, females, especially, Kathryn.

Cindy said, "You mean she is living with you in a house?"

"Yes, but she is keeping Paula. I cannot keep them in separate quarters. They both need me, desperately."

"I need you desperately also, and can't see how they fit in with us."

Kel had no answer and Cindy left the next day for Austin.

The next day after Cindy left, Lincoln was assassinated. It was a sad time for Kel as he had formed an attachment to the president.

Kel enrolled Kathryn and Paula in a private school that also catered to adults. Kathryn kept care of Paula who soon called her mother.

Kel wrote a long letter to Cindy explaining how he had rescued them from the Indians. He told how Kathryn could not read or write, and that he could not abandon them as they had no funds, and he felt obligated to tend to them. He wrote that he could never be involved with Kathryn romantically, and that he would treat her like a sister.

He got a return letter from Lorie. She said, "It will take time for this to heal. Cindy wanted you so badly, then you turned up with the woman and girl. It was just too much for her.

"I understand, because I know you better than my own husband, and I'm not envolved. Although no one can fault you for what you did. Cindy was so in love, that she could not stand it. Leave it alone for awhile, and let Greta and me talk to her, but slowly. It will take a time to heal. We still love you dearly, and I'm sure Cindy does, but it will take time."

CHAPTER 15

UNEXPECTED LOVE

Kel was invited to a formal ball were he was asked to play a few numbers. There was a woman named Erin Campbell there who was also asked to sing, and Kel was asked to accompany her. After their performances an orchestra played and dancing was being done.

As Kel was standing by the woman he thought it rude not to ask her to dance, so he asked her. She wasn't a dazzling beauty, but nice enough looking. As they danced she said, "My father told me something about you, as he had heard you play before, and told me I was in for a thrill."

"Well, were you thrilled?"

"Yes, you have a touch that shows great passion. That excites me."

Kel was feeling a bit mischievous and said, "Oh, in what way?"

She said, "You are a rogue aren't you?"

"No, it was just a playful jest. Are you with someone?"

"No, my husband was killed in the war. I was told that you have a daughter and a woman who lives with you."

"My you have investigated me."

"No, but my father knew you would be accompanying me, and filled me on what he knew about you. Are you attached to the woman who lives with you?"

"Yes, she acts as a mother to my little girl. However, we are not romantically attached."

"That is a strange arrangement. Is the mother of your dauther alive."

"No. That is why Kathryn takes care of Paula. My you are interested in me. Maybe I should ask some questions about you?"

They were sitting now and Kel said, "Are you a Christian."

"No, my father brought me up telling me that religion was just a superstition and that people with higher than average intelligence don't believe in myths."

"You mean like Gallilo, Isaak Newton and such."

"Touche, Mr. Keller."

"What does your father do?"

"He's a banker."

"Has he accomplished anything."

"Other than banking, I think not." She was now somewhat piqued and said, "Have you accomplished anything, other than the piano, Mr. Keller?"

"I became a cowboy out of high school as my father owned three ranches. After a year of that I had an incidence that soured me on that occupation, so I went to San Antonio and became a deputy sheriff. A year after that I went to college and then through law school. Three of my friends and I opened a law firm that has become quite successful.

"The war took me to Washington D.C. and I was hired as

a U. S. Marshal by the attorney general. I worked undercover in Boston solving a crime."

"My, I suppose your girlfriend was Joan Rydell, the famous singer from Boston."

"Yes, we were close." At this Erin laughed and said, "You know she died a tragic death."

"Yes, I know, she died in my arms."

This shocked Erin as she now saw he was serious."

Kel continued, "The attorney general became the secretary of war and he had me commissioned. President Lincoln assigned me to General McClellan and I acted as his aid.

"When he resigned his commission to run for president, I went back to work for President Lincoln. He sent me to the West to assess the Indian problem we are now experiencing, after that, I came back to Washington."

Erin then said, "What you have told me is hard to believe that a piano player has accomplished all that."

About that time a lieutenant in uniform came to Kel and said, "Colonel Keller, the president wants to see you."

Kel left with Erin's mouth agape. President Johnson said, "I just wanted to tell you how I appreciated your performance, Kel. It always seems to soothe me. I can't seem to leave my worries behind until I hear you play. It seems to make all my worries go away as if they were washed away with the music."

"That really pleases me, Mr. President. I would not have your job for all the money in the world."

"Johnson laughed and said, "That makes two of us. I liked my job when Abe was running things. He seemed to have everything in hand. I marveled over how he handled complex matters. No one misses that man as much as me, and now, the country. I'm trying to do the things he wanted done, as they were well thought out, and the best for the country. You having worked for him can probably attest to that more than most."

"You seemed to be doing everything that President Lincoln wanted to see done. Really I see no difference as you followed exactly the steps he wanted to take."

"Yes, but the country surely doesn't look at me with the same eyes that they saw Lincoln. I have many more enemies than friends. The only reason I keep going is for Abe. I can just see those big eyes looking at me expecting me to do what he did. I would never betray that, no matter what.

"Well, enough of that, let's enjoy the evening. I see you were having a long conversation with Mrs. Campbell. Her father is a Democrat, and voices his opinion agaist me as often as he can. Did she mention him?"

"Yes, she said her father was an atheist, and believes that people of higher than average intellect do not believe in religion. I pointed out a few that did and she saw what I meant."

"I didn't mean to interrupt you, go back and convince her that Jesus is Lord of all. I can't wait for him to return."

"I think he's waiting for you to fill out your term, Mr. President."

"Yes, as punishment for my sins. However, it's of great solance to know he helps me make decisions."

When Kel returned Erin said, "My godness what did the president want?"

He just wanted to compliment us on our preformances this evening. He asked about you, and I told him your father had convinced you into being an atheist, so he instructed me to convince you otherwise."

Erin said, "I don't know whether to believe you or not. However, I'm not sure either way about God."

"I think it takes many more reasons to not to believe than to believe. First you have to have an ego that says you are too smart to believe in God, when all of nature crys out to you his very existence. I can personally attest to the fact that Jesus is real. I have studied the Bible, and there are numerous times that the prophets have told of things that will happen hundreds of years ahead of time, and they come to pass. Just in the case of Jesus, Isaih told of him being born in Bethlehem to a virgin, seven hundred years prior to his birth."

"I was unaware of that."

"I believe the Bible is the holy writings of men that God instructed to write exactly what he wanted men to know, and has given Jesus the power to accomplish it all.

"There is a heaven and there is a hell, whether your father wants to think so or not, and each of us will end up in one place or the other. I ask you, if I'm wrong what have I lost, but if your father is wrong what has he lost."

Erin had a shocked look on her face. She surely got the message.

"Erin, I don't think it was by coincidence that we were put here together tonight. I think it is by divine providence. I think your name is written in the book of life and God is calling you to be one of his own."

Erin was awed by this concept and said, "I believe it, too. Will you help me to understand the Bible."

"I would be happy to. I feel this is something that was

divinely inspired, and I am called to fulfil it." They set up a time for Erin to come to a Bible study. Both Kathryn and Paula would attendend. Kel started with the stories in the book of Genesis.

Kel now did special assignments for President Johnson. Both political parties were at odds with him. He treated the South as Lincoln had wanted, and this infuriated the Republicans as they thought he was much too easy on them. The Democrats thought him a traitor to the South, so it wasn't long until impeachment proceedings occurred. Johnson beat the impeachment by one vote and finished his presidency. He did not even entertain the idea of running again with the animosity that was so prevalent.

U. S. Grant was drafted to run for president by the Republicans as he was widely popular. Negros were allowed to vote in the south and everyone of them voted for Grant if allowed to vote. Grant was swept into office with little resistance. He had talked with Johnson at length and Johnson had mentioned Kel as a valuable aide.

Grant interviewed Kel and liked him, so he kept him on as an aide to do special assignments.

Kel still wrote the group a letter each week telling all that was happening. He even mentioned that he was teaching the Bible and added Erin's name. This brought conjecture as to how she fit in.

Cindy said, "He's adding to his harem."

Lorie said, "You know that isn't true. Kel is as pure as they come. I think you made a terrible mistake leaving him."

Cindy said, "No, he didn't love me like I loved him. I

don't know if we would married as I want someone who really loves me."

Greta said, "In nearly every marriage, the love isn't even. Most men are infatuated with the sexual part, but that wears thin in a year or so. Kel loves deeply and the woman who wins him will have that."

"Yes, I think that is true, but unfortunately that woman will not be me," said Cindy. "He sees me as a sister. He did this when we first formed the group. After the first year, none of us could have ever been his wife. I have finally accepted that, and am moving on. I'll find someone, and if I don't then so be it."

***

Grant had sent many more troops to the West as there was an abundance of troops now. The railroad linking the east coast with the west coast was nearing completion and Grant asked Kel to go West and attend the completion as his representative. He had also promoted Kel to full colonel.

Kel told Paula that he had to go out west again, as the President was sending him. He said, "Paula, you can't go with me this time as you are in school, and must stay her. I don't know how long I will be gone."

"I hate it, Daddy, but if you say so, I know you are right. Mom will take care of me. Don't worry about me."

At the Bible study, Kel told of his assignment, but that the Bible study would go on as he had asked the assistant pastor of his church to conduct it. He had explained fully the circumstance other than that Kathryn had been an

Indian squaw. The pastor eagerly did this chore as he had met Kathryn and was drawn to her.

Paula and Kathryn's school had gone well as both were eager to learn. They did it together which brought them closer.

Erin had spoken to her dad and told him she was studing the Bible to fully understand it. He encouraged her as he said that she could then know first hand what a myth it was.

One day she said, "Whether you believe in God or not, there is a God and he has a heaven and a hell, and someday you will stand before him and be judged. You may not believe this, but what if you are wrong. Eternity is a forever."

This worked on his mind. About a month later, after Kel had left, he said, "Do you think I could attend your Bible study?"

Erin came into his arms and cried. She said, "Oh, daddy, how I love you."

Pastor Tom Long, saw his challege and thanked the Lord that night for the responsibility he had laid on him.

CHAPTER 16

LOVE FROM OUT OF NOWHERE

Kel enjoyed going west again. He wished that Kit Carson could go with him, but he had heard that Kit had passed away. It saddened him, but he knew Kit was with the Lord now and that pleased him.

When Kel reached the end of the line, he could see that they were making good progess and it would be less than a month until the construction of both east and west would meet.

He had met a surveyor who was employed by both the Union Pacific and the Central Pacific to complete the survey. He had finished laying the centerline and grade of the tracks. They were now slope staking the cuts and fills.

Kel was talking to a surveyor who had been hired to do the slope staking. The surveyor said, "Why don't you come with me and my crew, and get a close look at the work we're doing. I think we'll be through with this work in a week or so."

Kel had nothing to do but watch the construction which was now boring. Before leaving he asked a lieutenant who had a troop of twenty men about the security of the surveying being done ahead.

He said, "There has been no trouble in this area for sometime. I think the Sioux have gone north for the buffalo hunt."

Thinking the soldier had accurate knowledge of the Indian problem, Kel decided to go with the surveyor. They left in early morning and were there in less than two hours.

The surveyors were now well in front of the construction and Kel was with them. The head surveyor was Milton Wilbanks. He had a pretty young wife who went with him. Her name was Mildred, but everyone called her Millie. She carried water to the workers and fixed their meals.

Kel had an instant like for Millie to the point that he questioned himself if it were lust for another man's wife. She would look at him with her big blue eyes, and it sent chills down Kel's spine. No woman had ever done that to him, not even Joan Rydell who was the prettiest woman he, or anyone else, had ever seen.

She seemed to often brush up against Kel at meals. He thought this was his imagination and scolded himself for those thoughts. She was bright and full of fun as she teased many of the men.

Her husband, Milton, as everyone, saw she was full of life, and made everyone happier. Even though everyone thought the Indian trouble was over, Kel saw that everyone wore a sidearm as they worked. Kel instructed them on how to use it. The men were appreciative of his skill.

Once just after a shooting session, Milton, brought Kel aside and said, "If we were to be attacked, I want you to take

Millie and escape. No matter where we are, look for a place to go, in case of trouble. I know there won't be any, but I am a cautious man."

"If Indians appear, why don't you take Millie and do that."

"No, the men look to me, and I am their leader. I trust you, Kel. You are the best at what will be needed if trouble happens. Make sure you always have a saddle bag full of food and a canteen. I will tell Millie tonight, what I have told you. She follows my orders always, and will do what I say."

When Kel was in his blankets that night, he pondered over the responsibility that Milton had laid upon him. He didn't like the fact he was drawn to Millie, and being with her alone would be an extra burden.

What they didn't know was a band of Sioux from Sitting Bull's tribe had sifted south looking for isolated groups of whites.

The next day he looked for a place that he could take Millie in case of trouble. He noticed a narrow, but deep revine that was close by. He came to the large tent that was used as a cook shack.

Millie said, "Milton talked to me last night, and instructed me to go with you if Indian trouble begins. I already have a saddle bag with food for a few days, and a canteen. I'm glad he choose you, because I like you, and maybe a little too much. I don't know how or why, but I think you feel the same way about me."

"Yes, but I honor God's sanctity of marriage."

"Yes, that is another thing I like about you. You always do what is right." She said this with her blue eyes sparkling. She stood close to Kel, looking deeply into his eyes."

Kel said, "Don't do that Millie. I respect Milton as if he were my father."

"Yes, I feel the same, but I still like to look at you."

"Look, but don't touch." This made her laugh, and she had such a beautiful laugh, like the babbling of a brook that sings to the mountains. Kel backed away as if in fear, which made her laugh all the more.

Kel took the saddlebags and put the items in it into a back pack. He then rolled up four blankets and a pillow, and tied them up with a long piece of rope. He put in a trap for small animals.

Just like a drama that had planned the next scene, they heard the whooping of Indians. Kel picked up the backpack and said, "Follow me."

They ran to the ravine that was back of the cook shack about a hundred feet. They didn't look back, they went up the ravine as fast as they could. They had traveled over a half a mile when the ravine petered out. They were on a flat part of the side of a mountain. They rested, but Kel's eyes were always moving as was his mind. He saw a place they could ascend the mountain. It was a narrow game trail and rocky, so they went slowly.

They could still hear the firing of guns, which assured them that the surveyors were holding their own. They continued up the mountain until it was becoming dark. They were both worn out and hungry.

They found a small cave, but Kel was leary of it as it could contain a cougar or bear. However, it was empty. The pack rats had left a lot of straw where they had made their nests. There were no rats there, now.

Kel dropped his pack and said, "We will need some wood for a small fire. They both went out and brought back wood from a deadfall.

The cave went back some distance, and a trickle of water was seeping from the ceiling of the cave about twenty feet back. Millie put the coffee pot under it as they prepared a small fire.

Kel hung a small blanket over the cave entrance as a cold wind was coming up the mountain. He was happy that the smoke from their fire went back into the cave. Millie was already frying some side meat, and putting some beans on to warm. Kel checked the coffee pot, and it was three quarters full, so he took it and made coffee.

Millie was now serving them on the two steel trays she had packed. The coffee was boiling and Kel took some cold water to settle the grounds and poured them a cup."

Millie said, "I wonder how Milton and boys made out? I feel a bit guilty running out on them."

"I may have felt guilty, but then I think of what the Indians do to women, and know Milton did the right thing. I asked him to take you and go, but he said he had to stay with the men, as it was his duty."

"That's my Milton for you. He places duty above all. That is why I married him. I needed security, and he gave me that. I love him, but nearly as a father. When I saw you, it hit me like a blow to the stomach. When you looked at me, I felt instant love."

"Stop that, Millie!" Kel almost shouted.

"I see it hit you, too, Kel. We won't make love, but we can hold one another and feel the love."

"No! If I held you, it would be more than I can stand. Jesus said, 'When sin, comes, he will always provide us a way out.' I'm sure looking for it."

Millie said, "I won't temp us. I will keep a distance. I don't want to sin, either. You have brought a new feeling to me, that makes me want to follow you, and you follow the Lord."

That night they slept together, but did not touch one another until near morning when it became cold. Millie then hugged up to Kels back, and it felt good to him."

At daybreak Kel said, "I have to go back and see what happened. You stay here. You can keep busy by finding wood and seting out our trap. We will need more water. Our being apart will also give us a time to assess ourselves.

"It will take me a day, and probably a night to get there and back, so don't fret. I'll be back tomorrow night, but don't worry, I'll be back. However, just in case the worst happens. Make your way back to the construction. Keep close to the mountains. You can make it in a couple of days."

"I will always obey you, Kel. If Milton is gone, we shall become one. I feel a deep passion for you, and its not all lust, but of course that's there."

"We'll have to wait and see," and he left.

It took him most of the day to get there. He waited an hour listening, before he entered the camp. He could then tell the Indians had left. The tents were all burned along with all the gear they had.

The men had been stripped of their clothing. They had been scalped and their genitals removed. There was a ditch where he put the bodies. He held Milton in his arms and hugged him. There was a shovel with most of its handle attached, and he spent the rest of the day putting dirt over the bodies. He then covered that with rocks. It was midnight when he finished.

He went back to the ravine and spent the rest of the night. He had salvaged part of a tent that hadn't burned, and rolled up in that He didn't feel hungry as his gruesome work had taken his appetite away.

The next day he started early, but it still took him eight hours to return to the cave. Millie didn't even ask, as she could tell by his demeanor that all were dead.

She said, "There is a brook over there. I have some soap, and you'll want to bathe."

Kel just followed her and let her wash him. He was too tired to protest. He put his clothes back on, and they went to the cave. She had some coffee ready, and he sat and watched her prepare a meal. She had a rabbit that she had cooked. She mixed that with the beans and some wild onions.

Before they ate, Kel said, "Lord, thou has put Mellie and me together in your infinite wisdom. Marry us tonight as we become one as Millie said. Our love for you, supercedes all love one has on earth. Take Milton in your arms and hold him tightly, as he gave Millie and I life as sure as our mothers did."

Millie then came into Kel's arms and they kissed for the first time. They held the kiss in the rapture of their love. They then hugged each other, then Millie backed away and looked up at Kel and said, "I will honor and obey you until death do us part."

Kel said, "You are the one that God had for me all along.

I was nearly pressured into marrying another, but God found a way to keep me from doing that."

"I was married to Milton because of circumstances, and I'm glad I was able to give him the love he needed. Did you make love to the woman that wanted you?"

"No, but I was married to a woman who needed me badly. She gave her life for me, just as Milton gave his life for you. She didn't know she was doing so, but it came out the same. She came into my arms just as a bullet came at me. She took the bullet and I lived. So, we both had spouses that gave their lives for us."

Millie said, "I hate it that they are gone, but without that, we could have never found each other. I loved you the minute I set eyes on you, but knew it was wrong.

"I remember when our eyes met the first time. I knew I loved you. I wonder if Milton knew of our love."

"He may not have, but he felt something, as he could have asked anyone to save you, but he chose me."

"No, God chose you, Kel," and again came into his arms.

They found a way around the area that was safe, and returned to the constuction area. It took nearly two days to return as the going was not easy as they stuck to the edge of the mountains as they feared the Indians.

Kel laughed as they were walking and said, "When I was a cowboy, I had the best partner in the world. He taught me nearly everything I know about the wilds. He said, 'If you really want to know someone, spend three days camping with them.'"

Millie said, "It didn't take me thirty minutes to know you. You speak like an educated man. You use words that most of us have never heard. I know you don't do it to show off. You just think everyone knows those words. Milton had a deep respect for you. You never said so, but everyone knew that you were representing President Grant. It seems everyone likes the new president. No one liked Johnson. I think that the loss of Lincoln caused that, as no one wanted anyone but Lincoln."

At night they hugged close together and they both looked forward to that, so the trip went quickly to them.

When they returned, the construction engineer knew of the massacre, already, as scouts had reported it to him.

He said, "We knew that some of you got away as the bodies were buried. I see that Wilbanks sent you away to keep Mrs. Wilbanks from being captured by the Indians. I'm glad it was Colonel Keller with you, Ma'am."

"Yes, my husband asked Colonel Keller to take me to a safe place if trouble started. He gave his life for us."

"What will you do now, Mrs. Wilbanks?"

"Colonel Keller said that he would take me back with him, after the rails are joined."

A month later the golden spike was driven at Prometory, Utah. Kel and Millie had separate rooms at the hotel, but after the ceremony, Kel and Millie went west instead of east. They were married in San Francisco, and caught a ship going around the horn to New York City. It was a wonderful honeymoon that lasted twenty-two days. While they were in New York City, Kel bought Millie a new wardrobe. She argued because the price was so high. He bought her silk underwear and shoes she had never dreamed she would have the money for. She had her hair cut and styled like the ladies of New York City.

All were astounded that Kel returned with a wife. She was a beauty and especially with her new clothes.

Kathryn said, "I had a feeling that some young girl would put a brand on you before I could."

Paula said, "What about mother, I thought she was your wife."

Kel said, "No, Paula, she just watches over you. She knew your real mother, and being she went to be with Jesus, Kathryn took you. You will like Millie when you get to know her."

"Will mother go away because you have a new wife?"

"No, Paula. Kathryn will be with us until she marries. She will then start her own family. You and I will be together all our lives. Even though we don't sleep together anymore, you are always welcomed to get in bed with me. I love to hug up tight with you."

"I do too, Daddy. I will do that 'til I'm old and gray."

Kel waited a few months before he wrote to the group, to tell of his new bride. He now thought he needed to, as Millie was four months pregnant.

A house came up for sale at a good price. Even though it was a good price, it was still quite pricy. It had five bedrooms and two baths. It had a large library that was ideal for meetings.

The Bible study continued with Pastor Long still leading it. One night at the meeting he announced his engagement to Kathryn.

Kel turned to the pastor and said, "I see you didn't let any grass grow under your feet while I was away."

The pastor said, "The first time I saw Kathryn, I wanted

her for a wife. It took awhile, but she saw my desperation, and felt sorry for me."

Kathryn said, "It was a little more than that, Kel."

"I can see that, and I'm happy for you. It's an answer to my prayers. I so wanted you to have a happy life, Kathryn. I hope you have many children."

Paula said, "I'm getting all mixed up with all these moms and dads," and everyone laughed. She said it while she was in Kel's lap with her arms around his neck.

That night when Millie and Kel were in bed, Millie said, "I love you, Kel, but nobody in this world will ever love you like Paula does. When are you going to tell her you aren't her real dad?"

"Probably never. Why should I make trouble for her. Like you say, "No one loves me like she does.""

"You always do what is best, Kel."

Kel felt it was a good time to tell her about the group. "I have a law firm and I'm partners with three others." He then told Millie about how the group was formed and how close they were to each other. He then told about Cindy.

He said, "Cindy loved me, but nothing like you love me. She was the last that was unmarried and she wanted to be married and have children. I wanted more than that. I wanted a woman I was deeply in love with, and God gave me that.

"I loved my first wife, but nothing like I love you. She was more in love with her lust than she was me. She was almost violent in bed at times as she changed positions every few seconds. She needed sex and wanted it every night. Your sex is sweet, with love that inundates me as you saturate me with sweet love. I think that is what God intended. I am so thankful to God that he put us together."

"After hearing that story, I might turn into a Joan." This made Kel smile.

CHAPTER 17

A TRIP TO AUSTIN

It was the month of August before they left for Austin. Kel, Junior, was eight months old. Paula came with them as neither Kel or Paula would ever be apart if they could help it. Kel reserved a suite of rooms aboard a passenger ship headed for Houston. From there they found a railroad had been constructed between Houston and Austin. It was a one day trip, so they left on the morning train.

Kel had written his mother and Landon. He told about Paula and Kel, Jr. They also knew Millie was expecting another child. Landon and Louise were at the station when the train arrived. Louise first threw her arms around Kel, but then turned to Millie and said, "I want to hug you, so Millie came into her arms as Kel held the baby.

Landon said, "Paula, I'm your granddad. Did your daddy tell you about me?"

"Yes, Granddad, I know all about you and grandma."

Louise turned and took Paula in her arms and cried. She said, "My first grandchild. Please hug me tightly," which Paula did.

Landon said, "I brought my carriage, and everyone will

fit. A grand carriage was there at the station with a driver. It was Landon's yard man, Alvin, who was dressed in a uniform. Kel said, "Hello Alvin, do you remember me?"

"Of course Mr. Keller."

"None of that Mr. Keller, Alvin, you always called me Kel, and Kel it shall stay."

Millie was awed by the Landon's and Louise's house. She stood in the great room and stared. She noted the grand piano and turned to Landon and said, "I know you bought that just for Kel."

Maybe not just for him, but I told him he owns half of it. The other half is his mothers."

All had heard Kel play as President Grant from time to time asked him to play. He told Kel that his predecessor had told him to keep him as an aide if he did nothing but play the piano for him. He told Kel what Johnson had said.

Kel sat and played a couple of numbers then said, "That's enough of that, I want to hear all that has gone on since I left."

Landon said, "Your mother reads every letter from you at least three times. I enjoy them as much as she does."

They had a marvelous dinner served by the cook and a maid. Louise knew about Paula's love for Kel, so she had seated Kel between Millie and her. She had also bought a small baby seat, so it could be placed by the table next to Millie.

When they were in their room that night, Kel told how he wanted the entire family with him when he went to the law office.

Millie said, "Will it be awkward with Cindy?"

"No, I was told she had a boyfriend now and is over me. Lorie wrote me a letter and explained it all."

"They all love you, Kel. I surely didn't want Cindy to feel badly."

"Lorie said she took it in stride and now is okay with it."

The next day at the Law office, even though they knew all about Kel's family, they were shocked.

Lorie the most outspoken of the group said, "How long have you been married. Paula must be eight years old."

Kel laughed and said, "Millie and I have been married for well over two years, but I've had Paula for awhile." They all knew Kel didn't want to explain Paula in front of everyone and let it go at that.

Greta said, "Are you coming back to stay?"

"Not at this time. President Grant asked me to stay on, so I will stay until his term is over."

Cindy finally found her voice and said, "You've served three presidents, Kel. Quite a resume, I would say. Tonight, I will introduce you to my husband. I kept it as a surprise, but you more than out did me with your family."

"How did you catch him, Millie?"

"The first time our eyes met we were in love. It happens that way sometimes. Of course Kel would never show anything, as you know his honor." All three girls nodded their heads and said, "We know."

Grtea said, "But that's a good thing. He kept all three of us from going astray, especially me. Although our partner, he was also our father as we looked to him for guidance."

"Where are you staying?" asked Lorie?"

"We're with mother and dad of course. Their house is better than any hotel in Austin."

They ate lunch at a restaurant and Paula as always clung to Kel. They were waiting for their food and Lorie said, "Now say again, which one is your wife?"

Kel laughed and said, "Paula and I are very attached. We went through a tramatic incident where I had to fight to the death over her."

"Will you tell us about it?" Greta asked.

"Not at this time. It's not a subject to talk about just before dinner. However, it brought us together as you can see."

Greta turned to Millie and said, "Does she sleep in the middle or does Kel." They all laughed.

Millie was very quite, and just listened to the other as she could see the love between Kel and the three women. She was not jealous, she loved Kel so much she wanted him to be happy, which these women undoubtable did."

That night as they were in their bed, Kel said, "I would like to ride out west to see my father, brothers and a few friends. It would be too hard on you and the baby. Besides, mother wants to get to know you better as well as dad. I will take Paula with me, as I want her to have the experience of riding a horse and meeting my other family. You will get to know them when the baby is bigger. Is that okay?"

Of course, Kel. I won't say I won't be lonely, but I do want this time with Louise and Landon. It will be a good time for us.

Two days later Paula and Kel took the stage to San Antonio. The first night they stayed in a small hotel. The next day it was near dark before getting to San Antonio, so Kel rented a room for them at the best hotel in town. They had a fine dinner that night. The next morning about nine o'clock, they went to the sheriff's office. Sheriff Wilson was still the sheriff and was at his desk as was Harold.

Harold stood and said, "As I live and breath, Sheriff, your deputy has returned."

Both Harold and Sheriff Wilson shook his hand vigerously. Sheriff Wilson said, "I sure hope you're looking for a job, Kel."

"No Sir, I have a job in Washington D.C. and just wanted to show my daughter, Paula, my friends. This is Sheriff Wilson and Harold Wisely, Paula."

Paula politely shook their hands then returned to stand close to Kel.

The sheriff pulled over two chairs and said, "Things are slow around here, all but Saturday night, and that is much tamer than when you were here, Kel."

Sheriff Wilson turned to Paula and said, "Your daddy used to be a deputy sheriff here and the finest we ever had."

Paula grinned and said, "He told me about you and Harold, Sheriff. He counts you as good friends."

Harold said, "Thank you, Paula, now you're our friend, too." He then turned to Kel and said, "I'm hanging it up at the end of this year, after the election. I'm trying to get Herb to retire with me, so I have someone to hunt and fish with. I've about got him. I think if you'd come back and run for sheriff he'd go."

"You'll have to wait a long time for that. I have a wife and baby back in Austin, where my folks live. I wanted to show Paula all my friends and visit my father and two borthers. They live northwest of here the last time I saw them. They go by the name of Keller. I didn't tell you my true name at the time, as I wanted shed of them, so I told you my name was John Kelly, but it's actually Kelton Keller. Nobody knows any name but Kel, so it doesn't matter."

"You mean you're the son of Alton Keller? He's the biggest rancher in Texas, I believe."

They had lunch with both Harold and the sheriff, as there were no prisoners. They left the next morning for Marble Falls. The Mexican family that Alton had hired to help his wife, still lived there, and they were well received. Manual and his oldest boy wanted to show Kel the new whiteface cattle they now ran. The ranch was prestine. Kel complimented them.

Manuel said, "No one uses the house as Senor Keller never comes here anymore, except to do business once a year. He lets me do all his buying and selling. He even has Maria do the banking. He's like family."

They stayed the night, but were off the next day. Kel borrowed a buggy from Manual for the trip to Fredericksburg. They had to camp out one night, which Paula enjoyed. The next day they went through Fredericksburg to Alton's ranch.

As they were traveling Kel said, "Paula, if you are ever in a tough spot, the first thing you do is think out the problem and define exactly what it is. Without knowing exactly what the problem is, you can't solve it. You then try to think of the steps you will have to take to solve the problem. If you number all the things you have to do to solve the problem, you will have to put them in an order of what has to be done first and so on. This way, you can solve the problem.

"Life can be rough at times and I won't always be there to

solve them for you. You need to know how to solve problems, and this is the best way I know to teach you."

Paula scooted closer to Kel and said, "I love it when you teach me things like that."

When they reached the ranch, they could see several houses at the ranch. It looked like a small town. Kids were running everywhere as school had not started.

They went to the big house that now had six or eight bedrooms. It rambled all over the place as Alton had added one bedroom at a time.

Ceeley answered the door and didn't know who Kel was.

Kel said, "I'm Mr. Keller's youngest son, Kel." Kel had told Paula not to say anything about her grandfather in Austin, as he was going to introduce his other father to her.

Paula thought, *"This family is so mixed up, I'll never understand it. I'm glad we have Millie to keep it all straight."*

A wide smile crossed Ceeley face and she said, "You are the brave one who went to the Mason ranch to keep your father from trouble. He has told me that story forty time. Come on in and I will fix you some cool water. Is this your child?"

Kel smiled and said, "This is my daughter, Paula, Ceeley. Paula this is Ceeley. She has been here since the first cow came," and Ceeley laughed. Paula thought, *"She's probably kin to me, too."*

At noon Alton came in and was shocked to see Kel. At first he just stared, but then the recognition came on his face and he said, "Kel, is that you?"

"It's me, Dad. I came by to introduced your granddaughter, Paula to you."

Alton smiled and said, "You are very welcome, Paula. You

have several cousins around here. We'll go meet your uncles right now. They're in for lunch."

They walked out to another house and both Karl and Junior were there. They were ecstatic over seeing Kel. They both hugged him then shook his hand then hugged him again. Paula could see how they loved Kel. Both had married Mexican wives and they were both there and were introduced. There were kids ranging from two to their mid teens. Paula quit trying to count them.

They stayed two days as Alton wanted to show Kel the extent of the cattle he owned. Kel knew that Alton still had only one goal in life.

Kel asked, "Is Darvin Styles still working for you, Dad?"

"Yeah, I ought to lay him off as he's not the cowboy he once was."

"He's worked a long time for you, Dad. I would think you would reward him for that."

"Yeah, I guess so, at least a couple of more years, maybe."

They left the next day for the western ranch. They had to camp out again one night. Paula could hear the coyotes howling and experienced the wild west. They got to the western ranch about sunset. Darvin had just riden in, and he had dust from one end of him to the other. He at first didn't recognize Kel as his eyesight wasn't the best.

Kel said, "The boss sent me out her to be your partner."

Darvin was about to say he had a partner, but then recognized KeL"

He said, "I have a parner, but I'll shoot him, Kel. if you're serious."

They then embraced. Darvin then said, "Is this beautiful lady your wife or daughter, Kel?"

Kel had told Paula about Darvin.

She said, "Daddy told me you taught him everything he knows, so I figure you're his pa, more than the man in Fredericksburg."

"I see she got your brain, Kel. She knows an intelligent man when she sees him.

"Let me wash up and I'll tell cookie we have guests for dinner tonight. I'll tell him you're the bosses son, so he might fix something extra. I will say he's the best cook we've had over the years."

The next day Darvin found a gentle horse for Paula to ride and Kel and she went with Darvin the next day. Kel did a days work as Paula watched. That night both Kel and Paula were a little stiff, but they were really sore the next morning.

That night, Kel told Darvin that they had to leave the next day. He said, "Darvin, you're the best friend I ever had. I wanted Paula to have the privilege to meet you, so we came all the way from Austin to see you. This is probably the last time we'll see each other on this earth, but I just wanted you to meet my daugher. I'll see you in heaven, Pal."

They parted the next morning early and Paula said, "I cried when you said goodbye to Darvin. He will be my closest friend, too."

Kel brought her up close to him, and kissed her on the cheek. They returned to Austin and Paula said to her grandparents and Millie, "It was the best time ever. I saw all of daddy's friends and relatives. I have so many cousins that I could never learn all their names. My other granddad has a Mexican wife named Ceeley, and my two uncles have so many children I couldn't count them. I wonder why they live out there where there is nothing to do, when they have all those cattle they could sell and live the good life."

On the way home, Millie said, "I'm glad I had that time with your mother and father. They showed me what a good marriage can be if you work at it. I found out that Landon owns four pharmacies. They are in other cities managed by other men. The pharmacies are surely not his life, though. He spends a lot of time seeing that Louise is happy. The way they look at each other tells it all. I can see where you get your love of Christ.

"I spent time alone with Louise and she told me in detail about her life from the beginning to the end. She is so much like you. I told her about us and how Paula came to think you were her dad. She agreed that we should wait to tell Paula about her father and mother. She believes God will tell us when it is time. Just the short time I spent with your mother and father told me so much about you. I want us to live our lives as an example for our children to follow.

"What seemed strange to me was that your group still meets at your house. They love your folks, also. They let me attend their group meeting. They talked about you a lot, which told me they love you very much. They included me because of you. I'm just beginning to see how God blessed me by giving you a love for me.

"I think Paula makes me love you more. The way you two love each other is contagious. I want to provide her the love your mother has for you."

The trip back was on an ocean liner that they all liked.

CHAPTER 18
A PROMOTION

When Kel returned, Grant called him in and said, "Secretary Hamilton Fish wants you to be his deputy. That is quite a promotion. I told him I would agree if he would lend you to me anytime I had a need.

"Hamilton and I talked about it at length and we both think you know more about the Indian warfare than anyone as you had hands on experience. That seems to be well in hand with the amount of troops we dispatched since the ending of the war. He wants to expand your knowledge of his department.

"There has been unrest with Spain. Queen Isabella has been turned out, and a new King has been elected. He's a prince from Italy. There is still some unrest and Queen Isabella has not gone gracefully.

"Some fighting has occurred, but now it seems it has died down. We don't want to form alliances with them until we know more about the new government. You seem to have a way with people. We would like to send you to Spain as an emissary from America to meet with King Amadeal and extend our friendship to their new head man. I'm hoping you can find out the inner workings of their government so we will know who to deal with, and the plans for their new government. It may take some time, but both I and Secretary Fish have great confidence in you.

"We will have a formal ceremony when we swear you in. You have made a number of friends in Washington, and we want them all there. If this works out well for you, I can see this as a stepping stone to a secretary's position if I'm granted a second term.

"Just the little time I've been in office showed me the corruption in politics. You are as pure as they come, and I need your kind of people around me.

"I was pleased you found a wife. People want a married man in public office.

"Please spend sometime with Hamilton so you can obtain all we want you to find out about the new Spanish government."

The swearing in ceremony occurred on a Saturday, and a reception followed. All of Grant's staff were there, and all thought Grant had made the right choice. As always Kel was asked to play as everyone enjoyed his music.

Millie looked fabulous and stood by Kel through out the ceremony and the resception. Of course Paula was on the other side of him. The night went splendidly.

The next Monday, Kel went to Hamilton Fish's office. Hamilton had an instant like for Kel and said, "After the President suggested you to be my deputy, I was somewhat shocked as I had thought I would choose my deputy. But before I said anything to the president, I began checking you out with my peers. Everyone to the last man said I couldn't do better. They listed so many things about you that I was beginning to think Grant had choosen the wrong man for his secretary of state."

Kel said, "No, he has the right man. I also called on a lot of my friends who knew you, and they all had positive things to say about you. I think we will work well together."

They then started talking about what Kel was to accomplish on his trip. Hamilton said, "You know this is not without risk. Queen Isabella didn't abdicate gracefully after the election. She has her base, and that included a few generals. The army as a whole, though, went with the election. However, there were a few skirmishes after the election. It took sometime to find another king. They finally came up with a prince from Italy who was in favor of the people running things, and he only administrates their laws. I hope it works out. I would have liked it better had they called him a president instead of a king, but their culture could not stand that much of a change at this time.

"I hope you can spend time with the king and find out his thoughts of how the new Spanish government will work. Please also spend time with some of their parliament, or whatever they now call their governing body.

"Your task is not easy, and you will be there a long time I'm aftraid. I will want you to write once a week to tell me your progress. I found that it takes three weeks for letters to arrive from Spain, even if expedited. I'll be anxiously awaiting your letters.

"I thought about sending a military detachment with you, but after talking with the president we both thought that an friendly sign. However, if you feel you have need of one, just say so."

"No, I think you and the president are right. If I come alone, it will show our trust in their new government. I think I know everything we want to accomplish with this first contact, and I commend you for seeing that this had to be done, and done early in the new government's reign."

When Kel reached home that evening he talked with Millie about his assignment. She said, "I don't think I should go as you said there was some risk and Junior is just too small for such a strenuous trip. Are you taking Paula?"

Paula looked at Kel with big eyes. "Of course, it's a trip of a lifetime, and if something terrible does happen, we would want to go to heaven together." Paula clutched his hand, then hugged him.

Millie said, "I suppose that's true, besides I couldn't stand to look at that moping face the whole time you are gone," and they all laughed.

They left on a cold and rainy night. Millie didn't go to the ship with them. They said their goodbyes at home. The ship's captain had asked everyone to sleep on the ship the night before sailing, as he planned to leave at around four in the morning.

The next morning they arose at about seven, and could tell they were at sea. Their cabin was next to the dining hall, so after they dressed they dashed through the rain to the hatch of the dining hall. The dining hall was half filled when they arrived. They introduced themselves to the passengers around them, but no one had much to say as it was so early.

The captain came in and raised his hands, and everyone

went silent. He then offered a prayer for their safety and the blessings all had received. He then thanked and asked the Lord to bless the food.

Although the sea was rough, neither he nor Paula got sick. It had quit raining, so they decided to walk around the ship as their cabin was on the main deck. Paula had to hold on to Kel at times.

She looked up at him and said, "It's just like a honeymoon, isn't it, Dad?"

"Well, not just like it, but I do like being with you alone. You understand much of the things I'm doing. I plan to explain everything about this trip, and what I am supposed to accomplish." They did that when they were seated in two soft chairs in their cabin. Paula had countless questions, and Kel could tell she understood his mission quite well.

They stopped in the Canary Islands, and were able to leave the ship and do some shopping. Nearly everything Paula wanted was for Millie. Kel, smiled to himself as he knew that Paula loved Millie.

Their next stop was at Cadiz, Spain. They had enough time to explore that city. Kel told her that this city was the oldest city in Europe. It was founded by the Phoenicians thousands of years ago. He then had to explain who the Phoenicians were and their place in history.

Paula said, "I'm getting more of an eduction on this trip than if stayed in school."

They then went throught the Straits of Gibraltar, then into the Mediterranean Sea. They stopped at another port before reaching Valencia. There was a train that ran from Valencia to Madrid.

They spent the night in Valencia, then was about to board the train when they were approached by two men. One had a gun that he pointed at Paula's head. He said something in Spanish, and indicated for them to go to a coach that was near by.

The man took their luggage, and threw them into the boot of the carriage. They only traveled a short distance then were let out at a dock. They were taken to a small ship, and were now aboard it.

No one said anything. They were taken below, and shown a small cabin that they were put in. They sailed for the rest of the day and night. Their was a small bed that they slept on.

Kel said, Paula, just remember if we are separated, just know that I will come for you. Just be patient and do what they ask of you."

Paula smiled and said, "I'll look at this as just another adventure, Dad. I'll use my head. I'll be alright. I know you will come for me if they take me away."

The next morning, they docked at a pier. At the beginning of the pier was another coach. They traveled for about an hour, then stopped at a wayside inn and were fed. They were both starved, but Kel cautioned Paula to eat slowly. She ate at the same rate that Kel ate.

They spent the night there, and traveled again the next day and night. They were now in the mountains. Kel guessed they were west of Barcelona in the Pyrenees Mountains that formed a natural barrier between Spain and France.

They again spent the night at an inn, but the next day they arrived at a large chalet surrounded by a ten foot stone wall. The coach was let in, and they were ushered to a room with their baggage.

They were fed again, but in their room. It had a bath that was modern. A man appeared and said in English, "You are to clean up as you have an audience with the Queen."

Just to be obstinate, Kel said, "The Queen of what country?"

The man was shocked and said, "The Queen of Spain, of course."

"Is the king with her?" Kel asked. The man abruptly turned and left.

They took baths, and put on nice clothes. Soon after they were dressed, the man appeared again and said, "Follow me. When you are ushered in before the Queen, you are to bow and stand silent until the Queen speaks."

Kel whispered and said, "Just follow my lead."

They were led into chamber where the Queen sat on a seat that was on a platform about a foot higher than the floor. They bowed and waited.

The first thing the queen said was, "Who is this child?" She did this through and interrupter.

"She's my daughter and is with me at all times." The interrupter told the queen what Kel said.

The queen turned to one of her assistants and said in Spanish, "Take her away and put her in a room on the third floor." Kel understood most of it as he had somewhat of a grasp of Spanish when he was a cowboy working with Mexicans.

As a man turned Paula, she looked at Kel and he smiled and said, "Do as they say, Paula."

The Queen then said, "I understand you are an emissary from the president of the United States to the government of Spain."

As she had not asked a question, Kel didn't answer. He just stood there. The Queen then said, "Well, are you or are you not?"

Kel said, "Si."

"You are standing before the government of Spain." Kel did not answer. He just stood there.

The queen was frustrated and said, "Take him away." Kel understood, turned and was led back to his room. Paula wasn't there and neither was her bag."

The queen met with her advisors and said, "It will embarrass the king if these two just disappeared. We won't kill them, but we shall keep them so they can't escape. The king will then have to explain what happened to them as the ships log will show they reached Valencia."

***

Puala was taken to a place in Barcelona. It was a mansion that had many servants. She was told in English to never try and escape, because if she did, they would blind her father who was in prison.

Paula didn't believe this, but she knew no Spanish, and had no money, so where would she go if she did escape. She then thought of what Kel had told her about a bad situation. She smiled and thought, *"I will assess my surroundings and the problem I have. I will then think of the the things that I must do to help me escape. I will number them in the order that they must be done, and start my plan."* She smiled and said outloud, "Thank you, Daddy."

She then thought, *"My first job is to make everyone like me. I will smile a lot and do things that please these people. My next step is to learn Spanish. I know this won't be a quick escape, but one will arise, and I must have the tools to be successful. I won't try to get too far ahead of myself as this will be enough for me, now. I will try to look at this as another adventure and enjoy it."*

She was now about her business, and it didn't take long to learn who was in charge. A woman in her seventies seemed to be incharge. She catered to the woman who told her to call her Tia. Paula would get her things when she pointed. She smiled at her a lot. When they were together, she tried to sit by Tia.

After a week she began hugging Tia. She could tell Tia liked this, as no one at the mansion seemed to be close to her. A few days after that, she began picking things up and saying the English word for them. Tia caught on, and began telling her the Spanish name.

Tia saw that a tutor was brought in to teach Paula Spanish. Tia always stayed with Paula during her lessons and helped at times. In just a couple of weeks, Paula was speaking some Spanish. She decided she would never speak anything but Spanish.

By now Tia and Paula were together most of the time. Paula would even help her bathe. They became close. Although it started out to just be a ploy to make an escape, Paula began to like Tia as she showed her affection.

She had now been there three months and it was spring. The cherry trees were in bloom. Tia was now taking her to dramas and other funtions. Paula learning the city by taking in everything she could when she was outside the house.

Paula asked Tia to take her to the seashore. They took a carriage and Paula noticed the ships in the harbor and was wishing to see one with an American flag, but saw none.

They went to a cliff overlooking the ocean. Tia had brought lunch, and they pickniced. Their footman provided a table and two chairs, and they had a pleasant lunch.

They went shopping. When Paula was away from Tia, she asked the people who waited on her if they were loyal to the Queen?

Some said, "Yes," under their breath, but most said an emphatic, "no." She could then tell that most of the people were against the Queen and her autocratic rule.

CHAPTER 19

THE COUNTRY ESTATE

Kel was taken to a country estate in the Pyrenees Mountains. His best estimate of the distance from the nearest village was about fifteen miles. Everyone spoke in Spanish and he understood very little. He knew that he was over a hundred miles west of Barcelona. He wondered where Paula was. He then smiled and thought, "*She can take care of herself. She's a smart girl.*"

They arrived at an estate that had a rock wall of some ten feet around it. It was not guarded, but had an iron gate. The house was massive, and he knew it probably belonged to the queen.

His luggage was set out, and the carriage turned around and left. Kel's eyes took in all the could see. The first thing he noticed was there were no horses in the corral. They could be in the barn, but being it was nice weather, he thought that if there were horses, they would be in the corral. As he was about to enter, a big man frisked him before he entered.

He intered through a massive oak door into a great room that had a ceiling of about forty feet in height. The furniture was lavish. The first thing his eyes came upon was a grand piano. This made him smile. He was met by a maid who took his suitcase. He followed her up a marble staircase to the second floor.

They entered a large beautiful room that had its own bath. The maid opened his suitcase and put his clothes away. They then went back to the great room, and then into a library that was off the great room. The library had over a thousand books.

There were three women there, all in their twenties and nice looking. They were dressed elegantly, as if they were from the gentile. The maid introduced the women as, Pia, Lola and Maria. She then said, in Spanish, "Senor Kelton Keller is from America."

The women all stood and shook his hand as they were introduced. The maid then pointed to herself and said, "Lupe." The man who frisked him came in, and the maid pointed to him and said, "Alfonzo."

In just a day or so he knew the three maids, the cook and her helper. The meals were served punctually at eight, one and seven. The person serving Kel never asked what he wanted. She just set a plate in front of him that was filled with delious food. Some of it was strange to him, but he liked it all.

He spoke to the woman sitting by him and was able to communicate that he needed Spanish lessons. Thus every afternoon the women would teach him Spanish. They looked at him with leering eyes. Kel thought, *"These women were brought here to try and get me in bed. They would then have something on me."*

The second evening Pia played the piano. She was joined by Lola, and they played a duet that was nice, but quite elementary. Kel was sitting on a couch, and Maria sat near him. She smiled at him then sat a little closer. Kel said, "Is there any thing to drink?" He did this while acting if he had a glass in his hand.

Maria clapped her hands and a maid appeared. She turned to Kel and said, "Vino?"

"Si," said Kel, a Chablis if possible."

The maid left and returned with a bottle of Chablis and four glasses. The women quit playing and came and picked up a glass. Pia said, "Haz una tostada," and they all sipped their wine.

In a couple of weeks, Kel was communicating with them. When the two other women were not in the room, Kel asked, "How much are you paid to be with me?"

This mildly shocked Maria and she said, "We get two hundred peso's a week."

"Paid by the queen?" Kel asked.

"Maria smiled and said, "Indirectly."

"Are you trying to get me in bed?"

"Yes, we get an extra five hundred pesos if we can get you in bed and an additional two thousand pesoes if we become pregnant."

"Why don't you get Alfonzo to lie with you. I see him eyeing you quite frequently."

She said, "They would find out, as they are good at those things, and I would be sent to a brothel."

"I guess by now you know I will not bed you, but if I did, it would be you."

Maria smiled and said, "I know that, but I'm attracted to

you, and not just because I am paid to do so. I like you. The others do, too."

Kel said, "How would you like to make a thousand American dollars?"

"They told us you would try to bribe us. They would find out and my life would be the same as over, as they would cut up my face. No, I would not do that for any price. However, if I see a way to help you, and it would be impossible to be caught, I will."

Kel leaned over and kissed her on the cheek, but she turned his head toward her and kissed him passionately. She then said, "That was from me and not the queen."

Kel said, "I do like you, Maria. You have a nice quality about you that appeals to me, but I am in a bad situation. Did they tell you I was an emissary from the president of the United states?"

"No, but they said you were an important American that the queen wanted to hold for awhile."

"I represent the president of the United States of America. If I am ever released, I will take you to America if you would like."

"I would like that, but I have a mother who I have to support as my father cannot work. I have no skills, so this work is much better than lying on my back with strangers."

Kel never played the piano, but one day while they were having drinks he sat at the piano and played some of Chopin's music. He played with such passion the women were awed. Maria now felt a deep passion for him.

The women now begged him to play every evening. Kel

loved to play, so he played every piece of music he could remember.

He was allowed to walk inside the estate, but Alphonzo walked behind him and watched him carefully. Kel didn't know if Alphonzo carried a pistol or not. He asked Maria to find out. She did and said, "He has a pistol in a scabbard inside his coat. One of the yard men told me he is a vicious man who has killed several men. He is a patriot of the queen, and is said to be very loyal to her."

As Kel was walking one day he saw a pieced of wood that was round and just over an inch and a half in diameter. It was about eighteen inches long and was made of oak. It looked like a sailor's pin he had seen on ships. Maria called to them about that time as dinner was ready. Kel quickly picked up the stick, and put it inside his pants. He went to his room and hid it under his dresser. The dresser had a ledge just under it that seemed to be just made to hide it.

Kel noticed that a grocery wagon came once a week and brought groceries and other things the household ordered. A doctor came once a month, and checked everyone.

Kel began to think. If he could club the doctor, and take his carriage before Alphonzo could shoot him, he could get away. He asked Maria to distract Alphonzo for a few minutes when the doctor came again. She said, "I'll do it only if I have the opportunity and can't get caught."

He planned it for a month later. Kel had been there three months. The grocery wagon came, and two days later the doctor came. He was with Maria, and he nodded to her as they watched the doctor park his carriage. Kel left for his room to get his club and Maria went to Alphonzo and said,

"Do you want me?" and took Alphonzo's hand and pulled him into another room that had a day bed, and she shut the door and began taking off her clothes.

Kel was by the door with his club behind his leg. As the doctor entered the front door, Kel hit him with great force in the back of his head. He then took the doctors wallet, coat and hat. As they kept Kel in bedroom slippers, he pulled off the doctor's shoes. He then left for the carriage. As the two girls had just come into the room they went to the doctor. They had not seen Kel leave. One ran for a cold clothe, and the other tried to get the doctor to sit up, but he was out cold.

Kel didn't rush himself, as he had seen Maria pulling Alphonzo out of the room. He put the horse into a trot and the horse took to it. When they were on the road, Kel noticed what a splendid horse the doctor had. He took stock of the carriage, and could see it was the kind that the seat would lay down. It was covered and had rolled up material that you could lower in rainy weather or at night if you wanted to sleep there.

He kept the horse in a trot until he could not see the estate anymore. He traveled the rest of the day seeing no one. As it was getting dark, he saw the lights of village. He hoped that a store was still open where he could buy food and the essentials he needed.

He was in luck, as he saw a general store. He parked the buggy in an alley beside the store. He looked in the doctor's wallet, and it was filled with money. He bought many food items, a skillet, coffee pot, another pot, two blankets and a pillow. He had to make two trips to the buggy. Before he made the second trip, he bought a can of paint and a brush, and another hat. It was straw and had a wider brim.

As he was leaving town, he saw a pond that had wagons camping around it. He pulled into the area and found a spot where a tree guarded him from the road. He first watered his horse, and staked him out on some grass. He found some wood that another camper had left and started a small fire. He put on some side meat and opened a can of beans. He made coffee and by that time his food was ready. He was starved, but ate slowly.

After he cleaned his pots, he banked his fire and pulled down the seat. He then pulled out the blankets and the pillow. He slept until daybreak, He then took the can of gray paint and painted the buggy. He was noticing his horse and put two large splotches of paint on the back of the horse. He then packed up and left wearing his new straw hat.

He continued east as he knew that was the direction of Barcelona. He thought of Paula and knew she was smart. He knew she would be very careful and try an escape only if it were practical to do so.

He traveled another day, and just like the past night came to another village. He had everything he needed, so he passed through the village that bordered on a large lake. As he was passing the lake he found another camping place. It was a good place that was hidden some. He tended his horse, cooked his dinner and went to sleep.

The next day was like the first two. However, the traffice was picking up, and he knew he was getting close to a large city. He could now smell the salt air and new he was near Barcelona.

When he was in the city, he found an inn that was a little shabby, but had a place for his horse and buggy. He rented a room, and asked about a place to buy oats for his horse. It was close, and he was able to walk. He gave the horse an ample amount of the oats and turned in for the night.

CHAPTER 20

THE RESCUE

The next day Kel went to a clothier and bought a nice suit, shirt and tie. The doctor's shoes fit him well and were of high quality. He went to the harbormaster's office and asked if there were any American ships in the harbor or were due to come in.

The only thing that the harbormaster could tell him was that there were none there now. Kel was disheartened. He asked the harbormaster if he knew where he could send a cable to Madrid. The harbormaster gave him directions and he left.

At the cable office he sent a cable to King Amadeal. It read:

"King Amadeal:

I am now in Barcelona and need your protection. I would like to meet with you as soon as possible. Awaiting your answer at this Station.

Kelton Keller, Deputy Secretary of State representing President U. S. Grant of the United States of America.

The king received his message and wired the head of the police department to find Kelton Keller, who is the representative of the United States of America. He stated to guard him with as many people as necessary, and see that he arrives at Madrid as soon as possible.

The king had been in communication with President Grant telling him that Kel was missing and presumed to be kidnapped by the Queen. President Grant could do nothing but await the Spanish government to find Kel.

The head of the police dispatched a squad to the cable agency immediately. Kel was there and said, "I'm Kelton Keller, but I have no identiy because I was taken prisnor and my papers taken. The abductors took my daughter. He then gave a discription of her.

One of the men knew that the queen had an aunt in Barcelona and a young girl had been seen with her that fit her description.

Kel asked that he be given the address of the lady. The squad went with him. When they arrived, Kel said, "Let me handle this as I see my daughter. Paula and Tia were just coming out the front door and Paula was helping the old lady.

As Kel opened the front gate, Paula looked up and yelled, Daddy! Daddy! much like she did at the Indian village. She came running so fast that she nearly knocked Kel down. Tears were running and she gripped Kel so tightly his wind was cut off for awhile.

Kel said, "I told you I would come for you. I'll never fail you if its possible."

The police were there now and they approached the old lady and said, "We are arresting you for aiding and abetting a kidnapping."

Paula said, "No, she helped me. She did what she could until my daddy could get here. She is a wonderful woman who made me happy." All this was in Spanish and Kel was proud of her.

The police then backed off and Tia said to Kel, "You have a wonderful caring daughter. She has helped me so much. True, I am a cousin to Queen Isabella, but I only helped this poor child."

"Where is the queen now?" asked Kel.

"My guess is France as they will give her sanctuary because they dislike Spain, and will do anything to hurt our country."

They went back into the house, and gathered all of Paula's clothes she had accumulated. She put them in a valise and then told Tia she must go.

Tia asked, "Will you write?"

Paula said, "Of course, Tia, I love you."

The old woman put her arms about Paula and was weeping.

The police had orders to stay with Kel until he was put on a ship to Valencia again. Before he left, he gave the wallet of the doctor to a policeman and told him where the horse and carriage was, so it could be returned to the doctor. He wished he could help Maria for she gave her body up for him. He did have the address of the mansion and would see that she was compensated justly.

The ship to Valencia had excellent accommodations.

There were two beds in their cabin, but Paula slept hugged up to Kel. Kel thought there would be time to call this off, but it surely wasn't now.

At Valencia there were four of the king's men in civilian clothes, but heavily armed. The were in the compartments surrounding Kel's compartment. Their guards had wired ahead, and there was a large reception for Kel and Paula. Even a band was playing a symbolence of God Bless America.

The king was there, and had Kel and Paula ride in his carriage. On the way to the palace, Kel told of his ordeal and escape. He told of Maria who was instrumental in him making his escape.

A detail was sent to the estate and Maria was brought to Madrid. She was given a good job with the governing body. She saw Kel and Paula and thanked him. Kel said, "It is I who should be thanking you. You did a great service to me."

She had a twinkle in her eye and said, "It wasn't all bad."

Kel talked to the King, and several of the governing body on how best to work with each other. Kel was impressed with the king, and thought him democratic and for the people of Spain.

Kel had Paula at every session and told the men that he wanted her to learn everything he was doing. They all liked Paula as she had a winning smile, and was always curtious to everyone.

Someone had heard about Kel's talent, and he was asked to play for the king and leadership of the parliament. Kel gave a grand performance. The king then cabled the prime mister of England to make sure he heard Kel play the piano as he was another Chopin.

Before they left to go home, Kel dropped by the office where Maria was working. He said "goodbye, but she stood and gave him a passionate kiss. After they were out, Paula said, "I have something on you now."

Kel grinned and said, "That was for Maria. She did a great thing to help me escape. I will tell you about it when you are sixteen."

Paula said, "I won't forget, you know."

Kel smiled and said, "I know you won't. You may forget your name, but you won't forget that."

Their ship from Valeincia went to London. They stayed a week there and called on the prime mister. He received them graciously, and planned a reception for them at Buckingham Palace. Before they left he said, Mr. Keller, would it be too much if we asked you to play a piece or two on the piano. The king of Spain wired me to make sure I heard you play. Kel said, "Of course, I would be honored. I can tell my grandchildren I played before the prime minister and the king and queen of England."

They met the king and queen. It was a memory that Paula said she would never forget. She was then elated that Kel was asked to play. He played Polonaise and Clair de Loon. Everyone stood and applauded. They wanted more, so Kel played two more beautiful pieces.

On the way back, Paula said, "It was all worth it, Daddy. We both learned Spanish and had a great adventure. Even though she's not a great person, I can tell my grandchildren that I met Queen Isabella of Spain, the king of Spain, and the king and queen of England. How many people can say that.

"No one but me, probably."

The trip home was quiet, but Paula said, "Daddy, we had the trip of a lifetime. How long has it been now?"

"Let's see, we left in February and here it is the last of September. Over seven months. Junior will probably be talking now. I'll bet Millie was worried sick."

"No, Daddy she knows I was here to take care of you," and they both laughed. They told their stories over and over again to each other.

They were met by a band in Washington. They then were taken to the White House and President Grant, and four of his secretaries were there to hear his story. Just as he finished he said, "Paula has her own story." She then told of her captivity.

President Grant said, "You were a great ambassador, Paula. I'll see you are always sent with your father. He seems to do much better with you by his side."

When they reached home. Millie had a baby in her arms. While they were gone she had a baby. Paula said, "Have you named her yet?"

"Yes, I named her Louise.

Kel said, "Thank you, Millie. That is the name I would have chosen."

Millie said, "I thought about naming her Paula, but then there would too many of them around the house."

Paula hugged her and told her she loved her.

THE END

Printed in the United States
By Bookmasters